D0305505

ACCORDING TO RUTH

Jane Feaver

According to Ruth

Harvill Secker
LONDON

Published by Harvill Secker, 2007

2 4 6 8 10 9 7 5 3

Copyright © Jane Feaver 2007

Jane Feaver has asserted her right under the Copyright,
Designs and Patents Act 1988 to be identified as the author of this work

Extracts from 'Musée des Beaux Arts' from W.H. Auden, *Collected Poems* (Faber, 1976)
by permission of Faber and Faber Ltd. and 'One Art' from Elizabeth Bishop *Complete
Poems* (Chatto & Windus, 1991) by permission of Farrar, Straus and Giroux
Copyright © Alice Helen Methfessel 1983

First published in Great Britain in 2007 by
HARVILL SECKER
Random House, 20 Vauxhall Bridge Road
London SW1V 2SA

www.randomhouse.co.uk

Addresses for companies within The Random House Group Limited
can be found at: www.randomhouse.co.uk/offices.htm

The Random House Group Limited Reg. No. 954009

A CIP catalogue record for this book is available from the British Library

ISBN 9781846550423

The Random House Group Limited makes every effort
to ensure that the papers used in its books are made from trees that have been
legally sourced from well-managed and credibly certified forests. Our paper
procurement policy can be found at: www.randomhouse.co.uk/paper.htm

Typeset in Bembo by SX Composing DTP, Rayleigh, Essex
Printed and bound in Great Britain by
Clays Ltd, St Ives PLC

for Emily, Jessica and Silas

and for Esther

Under the Bram Bush
under the sea boom boom boom
true love to you my darling
true love to me.
And when we marry
we raise a fam-i-ly
a boy for you, a girl for me —
boom boom boom boom — sexy!
Anon

RUTH

1

We watched her from the bedroom window, striding along the edge of the road, tripping in the ditch, catching her balance, thump, thump, thump, her fist beating time against her side. She was almost skipping to get there, heading for the phone box by the cottages at the turn in the road. We could see a dark, muffled shape framed in red, in pieces, back to the world, phone cradled by a raised shoulder: Daddy.

She was talking to the door of the booth, holding out her hands to it. Daddy was all black until his head, still attached to the receiver, swivelled round showing the pale skin of his face. She began knocking hesitantly, politely, on the glass, tapping with her knuckles like Little Red Riding Hood.

Then, suddenly, a slap with the palm of her hand, and another, and another. 'Let me in! Open the door! Let me in!' She was jumping on the spot, crossing her arms and hugging herself. 'Get out! Just get out of there!'

We squirmed as if we were watching a film. *Mr Spark's going to hear her! They're all going to hear!* 'She shouldn't make so much noise!' I said out loud.

The heavy door of the booth was stiff, opening awkwardly and unevenly as Daddy pushed out, his elbows ready to lift around his head like a hostage. We saw a curtain blink in the row of cottages. It was too late to go and get her, much too late, she was already swearing at him, circling him like a little dog, backwards and forwards along the road.

High Shield is built against the slope of the valley as if it has pitched up at the end of a long walk and refused to go any further. From the road that runs parallel to the river along the top, it looks like a tiny bungalow; two shuttered eyes either side of a porch. But over from the opposite side of the valley, the back view presents a picture of how a house should be, on two levels, four crossed windows around a solid green door and the dry-stone square of a garden. It is a fixture in our treasure maps of the valley that include rabbit village, the bank of the reservoir on the horizon and, along the crease of the river, the chapel with its graveyard and trees and the jumble of buildings at Mill Farm.

There are four of us: me, Amelia, Biddy and Jack. In our family there are rules. We're not allowed to use the words 'cute' or 'toilet' or 'nice', not at home, anyway. We're allowed to say 'bloody' and 'shit', but not in front of Granny and Grandpa and not at school. The toilet is the bog. But not at school. And at Granny's it's the loo.

If we go out at the cottage we have to bring something back – wood for the fire, or gooseberries or mushrooms – otherwise, we get sent out again. 'Lazy bleeders,' Daddy calls us.

The bog is outside round the back of the house, next to the cellar. The cellar is a black, dank hole with a door that won't shut properly, and a pile of coal inside that needs collecting from. The air in the doorway is electric as if someone is hiding in there, waiting. We only go to the bog in broad daylight and even then, Biddy and Jack bang their legs against the wooden seat to warn off monsters.

Another rule: you're not allowed to pee in the bucket because it fills up too quickly. Someone is always peeing in it because you can clearly see turds floating. There's a shade of blue I can't see without the prickle of Sanilav in my nose – sometimes even the sky makes it run.

When the bucket is almost overflowing, there's a stand-off about emptying it. Always, eventually, Mummy gives in and we watch her, staggering out with the weight of it, muttering to herself that Daddy is a selfish sod. She digs a hole in the old strawberry patch and tips the bucket out, battling to hold on to the handle and aim straight at the same time, turning her face from it in disgust.

Strictly, peeing's supposed to be done in the garden. There's a burnt band of grass and dandelions by the terrace wall where three of us squat before bedtime. Every evening, if he thinks of it in time, Jack tries to catch us, arching his wee over the low wall to land at our feet, splashing up our wellies, or worse, onto our bare skin. Each time someone is tangled in their knickers, trying to avoid him, stinging themselves on nettles and shrieking as if the dusk was a room that contained only us.

Another rule: water has to be collected every morning by everyone, except Daddy. The water comes from a spring down the lane at the bottom of the hill. Mummy goes carrying two huge beer-making canisters with taps and we follow in a line behind taking bumper plastic juice containers. Mummy has the strength of an ox, Daddy says.

Drinking water is rationed. Washing water has to come from the rain butt outside the front door; we strain it for mosquito larvae with the tea-strainer. There's one stinking flannel and a pecking order for it, Mummy first. After a few days, we don't bother. Every now and again Mummy remembers and we have to wash our teeth in a mug of water outside.

Someone has to bike the two miles to Ellershead to get bread from the post office. The rest of the shopping comes from the Co-op in Ellersdale, five miles in the opposite direction, from the man who got a dent in his head in the war: all the things to keep us going, boots, matches, cereal, tins of beans, jam. On market days, Wednesdays, we go to Hexham.

At the cottage there is no one else; we hardly ever have visitors, no friends, and no incentive to be nice. We explore, we fight, we collect wood on walks, occasionally we bring bunches of flowers for Mummy to say we're sorry.

From London it takes seven hours driving, us wedged together on a back seat that smells of orange peel and the threat of someone being sick, eking out the fruit pastels, occasionally lunged at from the front by Mummy when Daddy says he'll crash the car if we don't all shut up.

By the time we arrive the sun is low in the sky and clear of clouds. Daddy has to put his shoulder to the front door; it gives way grudgingly, further impeded by a wash of three months' junk post. We clamber into the undisturbed dimness of the house, the smell of dust, of damp locked-up air. There's an odd shoe, abandoned from the last time we were here. Daddy strides into the living room and folds back the shutters, breathing in the view in an exaggerated display of being glad to have arrived, the sun falling on him like copper through the glass. Mummy stands behind him. She's already agitated because of the mice droppings everywhere, knowing that if she says anything he'll only tell her she's bourgeois and she will have to ask him why, in that case, does she put up with it at all? He rubs his hands in an uncharacteristic way to galvanise us, offering, after he's lit the fire, to cook scrambled eggs, at which Biddy makes a face and a gagging sound – the last straw – and he marches over, lifting his hand as a warning, the knob in the middle of his forehead pulsing as if he's about to blow . . . It is just at this point that the noise begins.

It sounds like a chainsaw at first and stops us in our tracks, as if the world outside is being cut up into the tiniest of pieces; and then, more purposeful, as if someone is engraving the hillside, criss-cross, up and down, a long word, like NORTHUMBERLAND, in block capitals, diligently, letter by letter.

From the living-room window you can see right across the valley, down to the river, to where the creature, half human, half machine is revving uphill against the grass like the nub of a zip or a fat fly worrying backwards, forwards, diagonally, looking for a way out, turning his hands on the handlebars, zzzZZZZzzzZZZZzzzzzZZZZzzz.

'What on earth . . .?' It was as if the whole effort of bringing us here, of believing it was the right thing to do, collapsed in the face of that sound.

'I didn't come here for this! Jesus Christ, what's he doing?' Daddy pushes us out of the way and has the window open, peering out. Mummy looks relieved to be distracted for a minute from her catalogue of unfit for human habitation.

As I fix the noise to the bike and pick out limbs and the shininess of a jacket, the thrill I feel at the presence of such an unexpected body is like a door opening in the sky and a light shining in. 'It must be the boy from the farm,' I say as matter-of-factly as I can.

Amelia turns on me instantly. 'Your boyfriend!'

'I don't even know him!'

'Why are you going red, then?' Amelia dances in front of me gleefully, shaking her fingers in my face. '*Lickins*! Got you!'

Daddy can't contain himself any longer and explodes with a stutter of instructions, 'Go and get the things from the car! Move! Out of the way! Go and help your mother!' He's clutching the top of a chair with both hands and his veins stick out like wires. 'Now!'

Mummy takes one look at him and I watch her biting her tongue. 'Come on,' she says patiently, taking Biddy by the hand and leading us all out to the front. 'Daddy's had a long drive. Let's leave him in peace.'

It annoys me beyond belief how quickly she rallies to him, how she's always in the end fighting on his side. But my irritation as I follow them out is tempered by the vision of the boy on the bike, giving full voice to my own longing for escape, and offering the sweet and unexpected consolation of a kindred spirit with whom in my dreams I might abscond.

2

By the second day, Mummy has got over the mice droppings, but she says she'd rather not come out. After breakfast, she sits in the kitchen with her hands pressed around a mug of tea and says she wants to be on her own.

The rest of us have no choice. And where not long ago I would have put up a losing battle so that walks meant being hauled along yards behind on the threat of no supper, now I relish the possibility of another glimpse of the boy on the bike, and I find myself being buoyant and helpful, sorting out boots and socks, hurrying the others up.

We are on our usual loop of the valley on the road that strings one end to the other, past the row of cottages by the phone box, past the Methodist chapel where I caught an old man once doing a wee against the wall, up to the letter box at Scarrowshield, and then steeply downhill, running dangerously hard in our oversized boots to the empty cottage across the ford and the raspberry bushes that sprawl in the garden there. Daddy hands us each a plastic bag. Jack is already cramming his face.

'Urgh!' Amelia drops a blob of fruit from between her fingers and then the whole bag and hops back from where it lands, wiping her hand vigorously on her skirt. 'They've got maggots!'

'Good protein,' Daddy says as she flounces off. 'No pudding for

you lot then!' as Biddy and I shove our bags at him and run off
before he can press them back.

'Girls!' he snorts, and Jack, who is filled with the novelty and
delight of finding himself in league with Daddy, shakes with
laughter like Mutley, on and on.

It is weirdly hot and still, nets of midges hung in the air and the
river glugging over its bed of stones with the noise of ever-emptying
bottles. As we thread our way along the bank, I concentrate on
walking, practising what I imagine to be an elegant nonchalance,
chin up, straightening my back.

Suddenly up ahead there is a clattering like a pheasant from the
path; Biddy is running sideways, flapping her hands around her ears;
Amelia is hurtling after her, plucking invisible creatures from
Biddy's arms, batting at her hair. Daddy, who is ahead of us, turns
and drops the plastic bags. He stumbles towards Biddy, white
forearms reaching out, face ironed into panic and in one movement
scoops her off her feet like a hammock. He lurches down the bank
with her, slipping in the silt, almost losing his balance, wading into
the river, knee-deep, plunging down. I can hear the low hum as
three or four bees continue to swing around them taking pot shots.
I am crouching, hidden from view; Amelia is in the water, too, still
plucking at Biddy's arms, single-handed.

Like an explosion, it is over in a moment, but in the air all around
debris seems to be falling and there is a strange suspension of sound
that collapses around Biddy, who is now out on the bank, dripping
wet and shaking with sobs. I try to look busy, scooping up the two
or three empty bags which are drifting off, inflating in the warm air.
Then I make my way down to them as if I've only just caught up.
'What happened?'

Daddy ignores me, bowed around Biddy, stroking her hair. 'All right. It's all right, Biddy. Come on . . . We must have knocked a nest. They've all gone now . . . It's all right.'

Biddy is looking straight out, head on a stick, snot streaming from her nose.

'Come on, let's go home. Let's get some cake, shall we? Teatime. Let's go and tell Mummy what happened.'

'I was the one who rescued her, wasn't I?' Amelia says, pestering him for recognition.

'Have you been stung?' Daddy asks with the concern of fellow feeling.

I blench. Amelia has a way in extremes of doing the worst thing, or absolutely the right thing.

'Biddy,' I say, 'let's see. Show me!'

Biddy peers out, as if she is looking over a fence, at each of her arms, inspecting the red punctures in their tiny inflated rings.

'Poor you. Did they get in your hair, those horrid bees? What mean and nasty bees they were.' Daddy is hugging her in the direction of the path.

When we get home and count, Daddy has nine stings, Biddy has seven and Amelia four. I, conspicuously, have none. 'I didn't see what was happening . . . it was all too quick . . .'

No one is listening. Mummy has Biddy on her knee and says we'll get doughnuts tomorrow when we go to Hexham. She is bouncing her like she's a baby, all put back together, and Biddy's loving it, being petted, fussing over the raisins in her cake. Seeing her there, pride of place, I find myself thinking half resentfully, half reassuringly, *See, they will stay together, how can they not?* It is not only Biddy but every one of us like a different combination between them that they would have to crack in order for either of them to get out.

'Those nasty bees!' Mummy says again and squeezes Biddy, holding on tightly, catching Daddy's eye as if to say, *Look, it can, it does work, it can be mended* . . .

3

If I hadn't been Ruth, I would have been Bobbie. The cottage always reminds me of *The Railway Children*, partly because of the endless games we used to play in the Railway Children dresses Mummy made us years ago that we wore, in the end, over our jeans, and partly because, in my mind, *The Railway Children* stood for the inevitability of things working out, which is how I used to imagine life did and would. It was the good version of our lives, the version without swearing and rows, the version where, given that everything came right in the end, the father had to go only in order for him to come back.

You can grow out of stories like you can grow out of dresses, but there is no avoiding them here, no throwing them off, because at the cottage they are kept like old blankets ready in a trunk, smelling their own peculiar and unforgettable smell of paraffin and damp. There's the story of our cat Clapham who we discovered a year after he was lost. He'd been living in the cellar without his front teeth, so convincing for a while as a monster that, until he turned up next holiday as 'Sooty' at Mr Spark's, we had to relocate the bog. Or when I ran away for the fifth time with a duffle bag of Weetabix and marmalade and only got chased because I happened to grab the whisky bottle too. Or the story of how Biddy nearly drowned in the reservoir, and how Amelia nearly drowned trying to save her, how the two of them were rescued by an angel of a man who plunged in from nowhere with all his clothes on and then disappeared without any thanks.

And until we moved to London, we used to come for Christmas too. Mummy got us to dress up and troop into the stable: Jack as baby Jesus, us three as shepherds, Mummy, Mary, Daddy, Joseph. We stood making our breath smoke in the lantern light and singing, 'Away in a manger, no crib for a bed, the little Lord Jesus laid down his sweet head . . .' every one of us, even Daddy, right through to the end.

One Christmas Eve we went down to the Burden's farm and Mummy carried back an enormous turkey, the size of a baby, in her arms, and worried how she was going to get it into the oven. And Jack and Biddy went with Daddy to find the branch of a tree, which we planted in a bucket of soil and stones and loaded with the ancient papier mâché decorations we'd made of aeroplanes, stars and hens still kept in a box at the back of the cupboard.

Once the snow came high as a lorry and we were completely cut off. No electricity. No milk. Daddy read *Just William* and *Treasure Island* to us until the snowplough dug a tunnel. Someone that year got frozen in the phone box calling for help.

Mummy had a thing about us eating for free. She had a book. She tried to make us eat nettle soup and dandelion salad. It was a bumper year for mushrooms one time – there were millions of them, everywhere you trod, huge mushrooms that sprung up like hoof prints all the way down to the river. She got us to thread them with a needle and cotton into long necklaces to dry above the fire or over the clothes horse, shrivelling to brown crisps, tasting of cardboard. For weeks she'd chuck a handful of them into everything she cooked. We took it in turns to collect gooseberries from the field with the bull. Most of the job involved scraping the brown mould of leaves stuck around the luminous ball of fruit, which impacted in our fingernails for the duration of the holiday.

We were brought up to be scavengers. We couldn't contain ourselves when Mr Spark told us that the cottage had once been a shop and Daddy suggested to us that the grassy mound next to the stable could very easily turn out to be a rubbish dump bursting with treasures from hundreds of years ago. It was quite possible for us to spend whole days excavating old bottle tops, rusty lids, potted meat jars, the fragile stems of clay pipes, even the head of a doll. If only we kept going, sooner or later, we believed, if we got deep enough, we'd find real treasure: ancient blue glass, gold coins, rings even. None of us ever wanted to be the first to give up. Old things, used things, animal bones, stones with meaningful markings, flowers pressed in newspaper and forgotten under rugs or glued unsuccessfully into the beginnings of scrapbooks: this was how we spent our lives.

If we went to Alston for the launderette we had the treat of a trip to Mrs Brown's, the antique shop at the corner of the square. Mrs Brown ran two crowded rooms, one on top of the other. Upstairs, tables were piled high with dinner services, chairs stacked precariously on end, coal scuttles and chamber pots under foot. Downstairs was hardly a room but a counter where she stood, framed with strings of lustre and wildflower cups; behind her, emerald and electric blue birds fanned out in a glass display case. She would pull out trays of precious mosaic brooches to show us, Venetian glass animals, ancient sets of solitaire, a picture of a garden made from tiny pink and grey shells. For the last few years she had anticipated our arrival, producing a cardboard box of broken bits and pieces from house clearances for us to take away — beads, keys, odd earrings, the head of a china horse — that we would rage and barter over in our bedroom, hours and hours of negotiation and tears into the night.

This time when we arrive I notice that Mrs Brown has Sellotape around her wrists and the blood shows through the tape like juice. She's talking to Mummy about where she lived when she was young, where she still lives. Then she asks, as if she has been thinking about it, whether we'd all like to come back later and see. Mummy seems taken aback, looking at Daddy indecisively. Because he shrugs (rudely it seems to her), she goes over the top saying we'd love to and Mrs Brown looks pleased, suggesting teatime and giving Daddy the directions twice through, illustrating the bends in the road with her hands.

It's four o'clock by the time we get there and she is waiting for us by the gate hacking at a bush on the side of the driveway. She seems smaller without the counter in front of her, as if she's left her shell behind, her huge face, more precarious; and when she moves, she rolls as if she's on board a boat, her feet splurging over the sides of her shoes. Mummy keeps hold of Jack and Biddy as we follow her and she points out with her secateurs the overgrown tennis court and the old croquet lawn. 'It was such a splendid time, summers here: visitors every weekend. There was always someone around, playing games, such fun! . . . I can still hear the chatter coming from round corners, over from where the nets used to be, can you imagine?'

The house has a wooden verandah, peeling green paint, and big windows divided into six like an egg box. The front porch, balanced on two pillars like a church, is filled with old Wellington boots and baskets of empty tin cans.

'Come down to the kitchen – I've got the stove going.'

Mummy is exclaiming at the house all the way, peering into the rooms on either side of the hall, how lovely, how well-proportioned everything is, 'You've got such beautiful things!' We pass in single file along a narrow panelled corridor that smells of brown and mildew, Mummy urging Biddy and Jack ahead of her, following Mrs Brown into an enclosed stone staircase, which winds down to a dim room, opening at our feet like a cave. It's packed, just like her shop, every surface, the table, the chairs piled with jars of different sizes, hundreds of them, with dull metal screw-top lids, each one filled with something dark. When she switches on the light over the table the ones round about shine with crimson, blood red.

'You'll have to take some away with you,' she says. 'I'll never get through all these . . . five . . .' – she's adding up on her fingers – 'maybe six or seven years' worth.' Then she takes a random selection, ticking them off around her as if they are the names of children. 'Plums, loganberries, raspberries, blackberries and cherries – all from the garden, we've always done it.'

There's nowhere to sit. She bustles towards the stove. 'I'll put the kettle on.' Telling us as she stands there how they used to go on cruises in wintertime, how the humidity turned the hairgrips rusty on her head. The dresses she had. The dances.

'It must have been an amazing time.'

'Oh, it was . . . you should have seen us! We had those great trunks, you know, like a wardrobe, drawers for all our things, hangers . . . calf-skin gloves, ivory combs, earrings. My sisters – my younger sisters – were considered quite beautiful in their day. They turned heads. They both married, you know. They both married quite well.'

She fills three mugs, squeezing tea bags against the sides of the cups with a spoon, making a leaking mound of them on the sink. Mummy and Daddy take a mug each. 'I'm afraid there's no milk. There might be some powdered stuff . . . in the back somewhere.'

'No, that's lovely – thank you.'

She looks at us disconcertedly. 'Would they like a glass of something?'

'They'll be fine, really, we've only just had lunch. Don't worry about them.'

'I've got some nice biscuits somewhere – Here we are! This old tin. That was my grandmother's,' she says, addressing Biddy and Jack who, unleashed, leap inside with their hands, scrabbling over each other for the unbroken ones, Mrs Brown sinking under the weight of them. 'See, I'll put it here, you can help yourselves.' They follow like pigeons as she puts the tin down.

'One each,' Mummy says and we hover awkwardly watching them because no one knows what to say next. Then Mrs Brown seems to shake herself as if taken by a sudden idea, raising her hand. 'Do you know, if you hang on a minute, I'll show you something . . .' and she's already off, shuffling towards the stairs.

The room sighs and creaks in her absence. There is hardly space to talk or move. Mummy looks at Daddy, raising her eyebrows, wide-eyed. Then Biddy pipes up, 'Can I have drink! I want a drink – I'm firsty.'

Daddy pulls her towards him. 'Shush. Just wait a minute.'

'They look like eyeballs – dead eyes, all bloody.'

'Don't swear,' Biddy says to Jack primly.

'I didn't swear!'

'Quiet!'

After a while, Mummy mouths, 'Where do you think she's gone?' and they continue in whispers as if we've been shut up in the dark.

'How should I know?'

'Do you think she's all right?'

'Bonkers!'

'I don't mean that. I mean now – do you think I should have gone with her?'

'It was your idea to come here. You encouraged her . . .'

'She asked us! What could I say! I didn't want to be rude! What could I have said?'

There's a scrabbling sound at the top of the stairs, a rustling, and Mrs Brown descends into the room peering at us as if we've multiplied since she's been gone. She's carrying a long faded cardboard box ahead of her, trailing the musty smell of talcum powder as she lifts her arms, shoving jars impatiently along the table to lay the package down. Then she raises the lid and gently begins to unfold tissue paper, grasping at something, holding it by the corners to her shoulders, shaking material down the front of her to reveal a delicate pale muslin dress, decorated with sprigs of blue and red flowers.

She beams at us as if to say, Well?

'It's beautiful,' Mummy says. 'Isn't it lovely, Ruth?'

Amelia is craning forward, stretching out her hand. 'Don't touch, Amelia! You've got sticky fingers.'

Mrs Brown's beside herself. She places the dress fussily over the back of a chair and then turns to fiddle with more tissue paper. This time she unpacks a limpid, black velvet dress with gathers across the shoulders and a tiny silver buckled belt. She holds it to her by the waist.

'Would you believe I got into this? Once upon a time. Do you know, I met my husband on that ship, second time around, the winter of forty-nine. He was a violinist you know, the *first* violinist.

But he gave it up after we were married, went into antiques . . .'
Then, impulsively, she says, 'Here,' gathering the dresses and
pushing them in a bundle towards Mummy, 'have them – if you'd
like them?'

Mummy gasps, 'Really? You can't!'

'If you like them, I'd be so pleased for you to have them. They're
no use to me now.'

'They're beautiful. Thank you. I don't know what to say . . .'

Mrs Brown's eyes are so huge they roll in the frames of her black-
rimmed glasses like fish eyes under a magnifying glass.

I wonder if all her family have died. I can remember her having
dogs, the shop smelling of damp dogs, two bull terriers Mitzi and
Taylor. One of them used to growl when the door opened. But they're
both dead now. It must be terrible getting old, I think, everyone
around you dying, and then falling out of yourself, crumpling up.

I dream going back in the car of a cruise ship, me wrapped in the
muslin dress, hair bouncing and curled, dancing clickety-clack to a
band by the light of the moon, watching the paper lanterns fluttering
in the sea breeze and the swell; or playing tennis on the deck, the
phut, phut of the ball against the racket lobbing every passing second
as if it didn't matter two hoots into the glare of the sky.

Mummy is stroking the velvet like it's an omen, like she's been
entrusted with something much more than a dress. She cranes her
neck round into the back and asks us, wouldn't we like to live there
all the time? High up in the valley? It must be true, she says, that Mrs
Brown is thinking of selling. Why else would she have asked us?
She was sizing us up. She wanted a family to live in the house, and
she wanted people that she liked, who would look after it for her,
keep it as it was . . .

Daddy is noticeably silent, but Mummy keeps on and on,

enthusing as if her heart has become set on it, so that Biddy and Jack and Amelia are joggling around on the back seat asking her if they can have their own bedrooms.

Then, crunching on the gears, Daddy says, 'Even if we wanted to, we couldn't afford it.'

'Yes we could. If we sold the house . . .'

'What would we live on?'

'We could cut down . . .'

'It was like Miss Havisham—'

'No, it wasn't! She's just old, the end of a line. It's the most beautiful house. It's my dream of how a house should be.'

'You're always after what you can't have – the grass is always greener.'

'No, I'm not!'

'What's wrong with what we've got now?'

'You say you hate going back to London.'

'But this is just a fantasy.' Daddy jerks his head back at us. 'You're winding them all up over nothing!'

'What's wrong with that? If you can have it?'

'It would be a disaster!'

'Why?'

'Because.' He says the word as if it's final, ignoring her now, accelerating out of a bend, acting like he's got to concentrate on the road. But she won't let it drop and keeps on painting to us in the back a picture of the life that we could lead, until we reach Ellershead and then she quietens suddenly as if she's unwound to the end of her string. She lifts her chin and looks straight out of the window and then round at him, glazed with suspicion. She's tried everything. He knows it's a test. And she knows it's his way of letting her know.

4

I get up later and later, burying my head under the tickling label of my sleeping bag, 'The Last Word in Luxury', to keep the light at bay. Right from the beginning, one of my favourite complaints to myself, because I was the oldest, was that I was beyond holding hands. I was the grown-up. Sometimes to make up for it I hold my own hand in secret at the bottom of my sleeping bag as if one hand were big and one were smaller and dream of what it will be like one day when my small hand is held.

When the latch lifts, there is no warning; it is like a gunshot. Daddy levers himself up into the room. 'Come on you lazy bleeders – up!'

The air rushes around as he bends and grasps the end of Amelia's sleeping bag, shaking her loose like a pillow from its case and her muffled shriek of protest, 'Gerroff! Leave me alone. It's freezing!'

'Come on – out! It's the middle of the day!' He steps over her heavily and I can feel the room parting towards me.

'I'm up!' I burst out of the bag. 'I'm up, I'm getting up!'

I earnestly set about undoing my zip until he turns on his heel. 'Two minutes or I'm back – with the flannel!' and thuds down the wooden stairway into the kitchen. I stop fiddling and prop myself on my elbows giving myself time to adjust to the upheaval of getting out of bed. It's like an air-raid shelter in our room, splayed sleeping bags, clothes and boots and sandals strewn. Amelia is whimpering and scrabbling about because a button has burst off her nightie.

When we get to the kitchen, there's already something going on. Biddy is whining, 'But I want to go. I want to go wiv you.' There's a lull as we come in and sit down as if we had never lived among them and shouldn't be there.

'Why don't you just take her?' Mummy resumes irritably.

Daddy speaks in an over-controlled voice, 'Look, we'll talk about it later. It's work. I can't take her – Biddy, you'll be bored. It's very, very boring looking round a gallery, you know it is.'

'I won't be bored! I want to!'

The pulse at the side of Daddy's head is twitching. 'You're not going. That's that. Now shut up; eat your breakfast.'

'Why . . . ?'

Biddy never knows when to stop and we wait with baited breath for what will fall, heads down.

But it is Mummy eventually who asks, 'Is anyone else going to be there?', blowing it like a bubble that shakes before it pops.

'Like who?'

'. . . That woman, for instance?'

'What woman?'

'Oh, come on, you know who I mean.'

'Tell me.'

Mummy takes a deep breath and looks around the table, indicating with her eyes that she can't say what she'd like to. With the pointed emphasis of explaining to a child, she says, 'The woman who's organising it.'

'Probably, I should think so.'

'Well, what is her name?'

'Does it matter? Dewar – it's Dewar.'

'That's not a name!'

'Her name's Helena, Helena Dewar.'

'*Helena!*' I snort.

Amelia says, 'There's a Helena in my class – she must be famous!'

I scowl at her, crushingly. 'It doesn't mean they're related, you stupid cow.'

'Cows eat grass, grass is nature, nature is beautiful, thank you for the compliment.'

She smirks with her head on one side and I'm consumed with revulsion for her. It's physical. I want to cram my nails into my legs. For some reason I think of yellow poppies: their warm softness, that soft sickly smell. Her skin. Touching her skin makes me burn. I can't bear to be near her. Her thick face.

Daddy scrapes back his chair with a plate in his hand. 'Belt up! I'm going. On my own. And that's the end of it!' The plate crashes in the sink and he strides out of the room.

'I'm going to the river,' I say to Biddy. 'Want to come?'

Biddy is sulking like Mummy, her lip out, looking darkly at the corner of the kitchen table. She shrugs, grunts and turns away out of her chair still not looking up and I follow behind, out into the garden.

'I hate him!' she says.

But as we get around the corner of the house, she begins a hopscotch and then we are racing almost on top of each other down the steps that separate the garden from the side of the house, and we break out into the lane, zig-zagging down the hill towards the lower field and the river.

She is singing now and collecting flowers from the ditch along the way, cow parsley and buttercups. When we reach the stile I catch sight of Amelia at the top of the hill coming out into the lane. I scramble over. 'Come on! She's following us!' Biddy fusses over the flowers and I leave her behind, picking my way along the path the cows have churned up, sliding down the bank to yank off my boots and socks. I step out hurriedly, stiffly over the pebbles, bending to roll up my trousers as I go.

The river water slices over the tops of my feet. 'Ach! Shit – it's freezing!' Everything in me rises. But already my eyes are skinned, sorting through the runnels and currents. We never tire of searching the river, and the spot just by the bridge is the best place where we imagine people must have come to hurl their old bits of china. There is a sort of Holy Grail idea at the back of our minds that one day we might find enough related bits to complete a cup or a plate or a jug, piecing it back together like a jigsaw. I bend and scrabble about, the water refocussing around my fingers, haphazardly making my way towards the bridge. All at once, I catch sight of something white. I prise a piece of crazed china from between two stones and bring it up to view, smoothing it of water.

The best pieces, we have long established, have patterns on them, blue or brown and white most often, smoothed around the edges. The rarer ones, an animal or a single flower, are the most valued and hoarded. This one is ordinary, a flat piece from a saucer or a plate and I skim it dismissively over to the other bank.

By now Amelia has her socks off and is making for the mouth of the bridge. I have a radar out for her from the very corner of my eye. 'Copy cat, copy cat, miaow, miaow!'

Biddy is sitting on a large flat stone with her toes just touching the water, singing to herself, 'Truly scrumptious, you're truly, truly scrumptious, scrumptious as the day that you were born. Tru-ly scrumptious, you're tru-ly scrumptious . . .' Amelia can't resist joining in.

'Amelia, shut your mouth! You can't sing!' The bile is rising like tears. Amelia carries on, head down, determined, and then sails into the moment I dread, hand fishing, jubilantly surfacing with a piece of china, blue faded flowers . . . She *always* finds the best bit!

I can't bear to be touched by her success. I kick out of the water, drag my feet across the grass in a futile attempt to dry them and scrape on my socks, my boots, stomping off out of the field onto the bridge. I am possessed now by the need to make it better, to find something that she'd want for myself, seething at the fruitlessness of my quest. I have no plan but the over-revved momentum of getting even and it is only as I pause to negotiate the stile by the chapel that a simple and obvious possibility presents itself to me.

The graveyard is off the path that runs along the river towards Ellershead. Dotted around in the long grass by the oldest graves there are small glass domes set like cloches in the earth, each containing a cache of booty: white alabaster birds, scrolls of letters, delicate flowers. Inside every one the grass has grown straggly, yellowish-white, like old people's hair. Some of the domes have been protected with a mesh of rusted wire; others are open and vulnerable as eggs, one or two, smashed by a stray marble chipping or a branch.

I had been here with Amelia not long ago time when, in one of the shattered domes, she'd spied a pair of sculptured clasped hands and greedily she'd begun to see if she could reach her fingers through the jagged hole. 'You can't take them!' I said, panicking and horrified at the same time. 'It's a graveyard! Something terrible will happen if you do.' She had turned to look at me and instead of defiance, I was surprised at how easily she gave in, pulling away her hand and reddening.

When I find the place, the hands are still there, reaching, where

Amelia had dislodged them, like a limb through a hatching shell. I kneel down and poke cautiously between the broken glass, my mouth watering at the prospect of possession. Through the corner of a cuff a wire holds them in place at the earth end. I twist and tug at them like a bird returning to a worm, until, magically, they give themselves up. They fit perfectly across the length of my hand, cold where they touch, light as bone.

Immediately in my head, there are chords striking, the Beatles singing 'I Wanna Hold Your Hand', the whole world shaking. I think for the hundredth time, if only I had been born a decade earlier, I could have been a teenager in the sixties, so that I could have married Ray Davies or Keith Richards or Bob Dylan. It takes me whole mornings to tape the songs from Daddy's old records – the Beatles, the Kinks, the Rolling Stones, the Who – songs that will keep me attached to the world when we come here. Daddy isn't even interested in music any longer, but he was when I was little. And those are the songs that I remember and keep playing. It seemed darker in those days, but it was a warm kind of dark, safer and surer. He trained me to sit by the record player and chose the songs by their sleeves for him to work along to, full blast over the typewriter, one after the other until lunchtime or teatime. And now all those words I've known by heart have begun to mean something, to make sense, speaking to me about how a life could be where there is real love and real feeling. I can sing along in my head with every accompaniment, every nuance in place, every falter, every delayed beat. And those drums, the bass guitar, strike something right in my spinal chord: the whole sum of my human existence, everything I feel I want, that is missing, is there.

My skin is tingling as I post the hands into the pouch at the front of my jumper. I can't take them back to the cottage. Instead, when I get to the steps at the top of the lane, I keep going, round to where I can climb the wall into the big triangle of overgrown garden. Then I make for the far corner where the nettles have been flattened to a seat-sized patch hedged in by hawthorn, an outpost from which it's possible to spy on the whole valley.

Sitting absolutely still, waiting for the hum in the air to settle, I can hear Biddy and Jack in the front garden. They are climbing onto the seat of the swing and start to sing as they bend their knees alternately, cranking up, 'Under the Bam Bush, Under the sea boom boom boom, true love to you my darling, true love to me . . .

'Bram,' I can't help correcting, under my breath, 'brram.' I hate their missing 'r'; it makes me bite my tongue, just as bad as hearing chalk scratching on board, or cardboard across carpet and I have to say it out loud to put the 'r' back in.

'And when we marry, we raise a fam-i-ly' – I search as far as I can see, just in case Amelia has been following me. But there's nothing except the swing – 'a boy for you, a girl for me, boom, boom, boom, boom – SEXY!' – and the blur of the river further off. The old toy trowel is still by the wall from where we have been digging on and off and I fetch it over to scrape a hollow in the dry soil, positioning the hands carefully and then scrabbling earth back over to bury them, pulling the long grasses around.

When I climb back out of the garden, I wait for a second near the gate, scratching at the midge bites on my elbow. Biddy and Jack are still jangling on the swing, but otherwise it seems almost unnaturally quiet. No typing. I step between the cracks of the flagstone path and in at the back door, lifting my head out of habit to listen at the bottom of the stairs. I hadn't particularly expected to hear anything, certainly not the forced, hushed voices that reach my ears now, squeezed out from behind the door of the living room. So instead of going straight on into the kitchen I stop, as if in mid-flight, ready to move the moment I am discovered.

'. . . I just can't bear this. Please don't be so cold. Don't be like this.'

'Like what?'

'You know what I mean — as if you're not here. I'd rather you *weren't* here, than like this. I just can't bear it.'

There's a long pause and then Daddy, even quieter, 'Maybe I should've stayed in London.'

'What do you mean?'

'Maybe it was bound not to work.'

'How can you say that?'

'I just can't seem to give you what you want.'

'You don't know what I want.'

'We're going round in circles — can't you just leave it, let things be for a while?'

'It would be all right if you loved me. You've said you love me, well prove it — you can't, can you?'

'You don't realise how difficult it is for *me*.'

There's silence and then the clutter-thud of an object, a book maybe, landing. 'You fucking bastard! You shit. You fucking shit!'

And then there's a terrible wail that seems to go on and on until it breaks into a soft, low keening. It stops. 'Get out! Just get out!' And then again it comes, animal and miserable.

Daddy bursts out of the door and down the stairs before I have a chance to disappear. He smells as if he is on fire as he shoves past me and off round the corner. I hear him up the steps at the side of the house, two at a time rattling his keys, then the car door slamming, the engine turning lugubriously, stuttering, stalling, starting again, pumped to a fierce roar and then a screech of tyres and the spitting of stones.

When I go outside Biddy and Jack are standing face to face hardly moving. The spell is broken by the fidget of the swing and the renewed sound of sobbing upstairs, like the sea, mumbling over and over, 'How can he? How can he do it? How could he? How can he be such a bastard?' round and round.

The swing lurches into action again, as if nothing has happened. Biddy is singing, 'You stay in my house, I'll stay in your house, do-de-do-do, do-de-do-do.'

And Jack answers, giggling, 'You sleep in my bed, I'll sleep in your bed.'

'No,' says Biddy, getting louder. 'Listen: I'll wee in your bed, you wee in my bed, do-de-do-do.'

Jack is crippled with laughter and can hardly stand up straight. 'Wait . . . I'll pick your nose, you pick my nose—' They both collapse.

'Shut up!' I screech at them. 'Everyone can hear! Do you want the police to come? Just shut up!'

5

Two days after that it was raining, splattering against the pane like gravel and then like kisses. Rainy days were the worst; it was always an effort to get up, knowing everyone would be buzzing about, cooped in.

Biddy was pulling on footballer socks and tucking her jeans into the tops of them. 'Do you think he'll come back?'

'Of course he will.'

'What if he doesn't?'

'He will.'

'Why's Mummy crying then?'

'She isn't *still* crying . . .'

'She is. I can hear her.'

I tried to listen, but couldn't hear anything except the rain pattering at the window. 'It's the rain.'

'Will they get a divorce?'

'No.'

'Will Jack go and live with Daddy?'

'Shut up. He's coming back. He always comes back.'

Amelia had turned around in her sleeping bag like a slug. 'You have to go and live in a council flat if you get divorced.'

Biddy lights up. 'I want to live in a flat.'

'With rats in it?'

'We could have a cat.'

I was out of bed, already half dressed. None of us took all our clothes off for bed. 'Look. They're not getting divorced.'

'Why's Mummy crying then?'

'She's not.'

'She is!'

Amelia could go on all day. It was like origami, at which she excelled, all those folds, pernickety tucks and refolds. She didn't seem to have a sense of boredom. I stepped over her disdainfully on my way to the door and set off downstairs to the kitchen.

I heard the noise before I saw anything, a furious *scritch, scratch, scritch-scritch*. When I got into the room I saw her, the back of her, on her knees with her head deep in the oven. She was still wearing her nightie and her feet were bare, heels cracked and purplish as if she'd been walking in paint. It looked for a moment as if she was going to climb all the way inside, as if she had a teaspoon in there and was scratching and digging to find a way out. Then I watched as her hand reached out behind her and she shook a ragged green scourer over the bowl of water next to her foot, immersed and squeezed it out before drawing it back inside.

I don't remember the oven ever being cleaned. I turned around like a spaceman so she wouldn't hear me and crept back up the stairs.

'Is he back?' Biddy asked.

I looked around for distractions. 'Do you want to do a recording?'

I'd brought Mummy's tape recorder with us so I could play my tapes. Looking for paper one day, I'd come across the old microphone and lead buried at the bottom of Daddy's desk, and by a long process of trial and error had worked out how we could record ourselves.

I wasn't going to let anyone else in on the trick and I was very sparing with the treat of recording; it would generally guarantee cooperation from Biddy or Jack. Biddy was already excited, pressing her hands together. 'Can we do Blondie?'

'Not again! You're obsessed with Blondie.'

'No, I'm not!'

'Let's do "Things We Said Today"!'

'You're *obthethed*—'

'Don't use words you can't even pronounce! Do you want to do it, or not?!'

We'd been practising the harmonies by singing the song over and over in the back of the car on the way to Alston last time and we'd recorded one version already with Biddy introducing us, '*And now, by popular command*—'

'*Demand!*'

'*The wonderful, the talented, let's hear it for the*— Can I do the top bit?'

'OK, OK. Hang on a minute.' I was rewinding the tape with a biro because the plastic knob on the rewind button had broken off.

'Right – one, two, three, four . . .' and then I pressed the play and the red buttons firmly together, nodding her in. It took a while for us to settle on the same notes. Just as we got there and were preparing to divide, Amelia cut in,

'Can I do it?' I don't know why she bothered to ask. I was shaking my head violently over our singing.

And then we were about to embark into out favourite bit, the middle section, which we'd perfected as a rough and ready tribute to Elvis, when Amelia snatched the microphone from me, pulling the cord out of its socket.

'Amelia! Give it back! You can't sing!'

'It's my turn!'

'We're not having turns. Give it back. It was our idea!'

'Hard cheese!'

'Give it back, fat cow!'

'Cows eat grass, grass is nature, th—'

'Fuck off!'

Biddy was beside herself, 'I'll tell of you!'

'Go and tell!'

'Give it back.'

'Make me!' Amelia held it high above her head and I knew I couldn't bring myself to touch her to get it.

But while she was sneering at me, Biddy stretched up behind her and snatched it back and for two seconds was skipping around in glee. Incensed, Amelia grabbed Biddy's arm, bringing her head inexorably towards it, biting into the chunky flesh like an apple and as Biddy watched her she let out a cry of dismay. Amelia wouldn't let go.

Suddenly there was a scream from the bottom of the stairs, 'What on earth is going on? I can't leave you for a second! If I have to come up there I'll kill someone!'

Biddy had taken her arm back and was cradling it in horror. There was a clear circular mark like a biscuit cutter, but no blood. Amelia was defiant. She was breathing heavily and shoved her feet into her boots. 'Who wants to play your poxy game, anyway?' She flounced out, scraping the front door across the lino, bringing it stuttering to a close behind her.

'What a bitch!' I said, delighted that Amelia had so spectacularly lived up to my worst depiction of her.

The threat hung like a question in the air. Biddy was whimpering and didn't look as if she would budge. 'Come on. Why don't we go

out?' And then I had an idea to tempt her. 'Biddy, if you want, I'll
show you something, something really secret – if you promise,
absolutely promise, not to tell.'

Biddy switched off her tears and her face brightened with
curiosity.

'I really mean it, though, you've got to swear not to tell.'

'I won't.'

'Swear.'

'Cross my heart, hope to die.'

'OK then, come on.'

I took her out the front way, double-checking that Amelia had
vanished, and then we climbed over the lower part of the wall to the
wild bit of the garden. Even as we headed there I had a nagging
doubt, but it felt too late. 'Promise on your life,' I said.

Biddy was nodding eagerly. 'I did already.'

The stolen hands had been bothering me like a bruise and part of
me felt, by sharing the secret, I could spread the responsibility. I
pushed back the grass and two stray nettle heads with the trowel and
then began rummaging in the soil.

'What is it?' Biddy was hunched down against me, peering over
my shoulder. 'Is it treasure?'

'No. Wait.'

The soil was still loose round about and the hands came away,
spilling crumbs of grit from the hole in one cuff and the orange
thread of a centipede.

'It's from the graveyard!' Biddy cried straight out with all the
force of something significant and something forbidden that
instantly made me regret showing her.

'How do you know?'

'I've seen it there.'

I had to think quickly. 'I found them . . . in the river. I found them when we were looking for china. So . . . I brought them here. To keep them safe.'

'They're from the graveyard.'

'I know! All right. I can see that. But I found them in the river.'

'Are they from dead people?'

God, why did I even think of showing her! Now I'd fired something off in her head, she'd never manage to keep it quiet. But I kept my cool and felt my way slowly back from the point at which I could imagine her running and telling all the way home.

'If they're from the graveyard – yes, all right, they are! Then maybe what we'd better do is put them back.'

'Don't you want to keep them?'

Already she was beginning to implicate herself in the decision and I was pleased at the way I'd inveigled her as if I'd secured a buyer for the *Mona Lisa*. 'We can't keep them if they come from the graveyard, can we?'

Before she could think about it we heard a rustle from the steps on the lane and I grabbed her. 'You swore not to tell, remember. You mustn't tell.'

It wasn't Amelia, it was Jack trying to hop up the stairs. I pushed the hands hurriedly back into the soil and stood up with her so we could just see the top of his head. 'Jack!' I called. 'Where've you been?'

He looked up. 'What are you doing?'

'Nothing. We're coming back. We're hungry.'

Biddy had kept quiet and I was pleased that she seemed to be on my side and she, no doubt, was pleased to be part of a plot that Jack was not.

*

When we got round to the back door, it was open and I could still hear the grating scritch-scratch of metal. 'When's dinner?' Biddy asked. 'Can I have a biscuit, Mummy?'

There was no reply.

'Where's Daddy?' And then, she said accusingly, 'Ruth says you're going to get a divorce.'

I pushed into the kitchen behind her. 'I did not!'

Mummy lifted her head out of the oven and turned on her knees and held her arms out towards Biddy. 'Why on earth did you say that to her?'

'I didn't say it. She's lying!'

'I'm not lying.' Biddy looked directly at me in a way that made me check myself.

'It was a very silly thing to say.' Mummy was rubbing Biddy's back. 'Everyone has fights sometimes, don't they? You and Jack, Ruth and Amelia. But you still love each other.'

No! She had no idea of the game I played where Biddy, Jack and Amelia were strung above a pool of crocodiles to see which one of them I'd let fall first.

Mummy had turned her back on me, collecting herself from the floor. And I left it. If I dug any further, who knows what Biddy might have said.

6

He did come back. It served him right because he came back the same day that man Marcus had walked all the way to see us from Bridge End and Mummy had asked him in for tea and Amelia gave him the scarf that was meant for Daddy, and then Mummy drank wine, which he always hated.

I was pleased to have been proven right, again; but I was annoyed too. Although she was cross with him and they had a row, by the next morning she was conciliatory. She chattered over us as if we didn't exist and, having felt sorry for her, I now despised her for giving in so easily, for letting it seem as if nothing at all had happened.

Later, they announced they were going off on their own and Mummy was even giggling as though they had something secret planned. *That's the last time I'll ever believe anything is wrong!*

When they'd gone, Amelia, Biddy and I were milling about upstairs, falling over each other, quarrelling about who had the chair and who had the window. Amelia with her customary physical excess had begun wrestling the chair from me, scraping it across the floor, rucking up the carpet. Biddy was squatting on the deep sill and sorting through the Happy Family cards, swapping wives and husbands and brothers and sisters when suddenly we were startled by the sound of something falling thunderously outside.

'Hey! Look at him!' Biddy yelped, jumping to her knees with her hands up against the glass.

'Don't lean on the window — you'll fall out!' I was right behind her.

'Look! Look at him!'

I craned forward. In the field below the cottage down by the ruined barn was a figure, bare from the waist up, skin shining like a lamp against the greenness of the field.

It was the boy from the farm.

There had been two boys, Robert and Daniel they were called, but the younger one, Daniel, died. It must have been not last summer, but the one before, when we all had to come back to London early because Daddy had needed to go to Germany to review an exhibition and Mummy didn't like driving back all the way on her own. We only found out the next Christmas that he'd been squashed under a tractor. Maybe because it had already happened it didn't really sink in, or maybe it was just because we didn't really know them. Once, when we were much younger, we had tea at the farmhouse and nobody spoke. Another time, later, we'd spied on the two of them from behind walls as if they were a different species. But we never played with them.

'Your boyfriend.' Amelia leered at me.

Biddy had her nose against the glass. 'I can see his titties!'

'Boys don't have tits — you shouldn't be looking.'

'You're looking!'

He was clambering along the tops of the thick walls with a long hammer, steadying himself upright, heaving it up above his head and, with a yell, down against the stone to the side of him, kicking at the loose bits, bending down to dislodge them with his hands. Chips of stone flew like sparks and larger stones wobbled and toppled to the bed of nettles below him; dust rose up like smoke around his ears.

'Let's go outside!' Biddy was already clambering down from the window. It was hard not to catch the thrill of energy that rose off him, like a heat haze that you could see and smell. He looked like a gladiator performing in a ring.

Amelia had her arms folded as if to say *I told you so*, 'Off to see your boyfriend, then!' I followed Biddy out into the garden and into Jack's den in the hedge, which gave a perfect view over the lane and the gate into the field. Jack was rattling on the swing.

'Hey, get out of there!'

Biddy turned and made a face. 'Make me!'

Nowadays Jack spends most of his days at the farm. At first Mummy wouldn't let him go; she tried to divert him by thinking up things to do at home, giving him a patch of the garden to grow carrots and radishes. But he was impossible to keep still and in the end she had to give in, telling him, whenever she caught him, to be careful, how easy it was to have an accident on a farm, to stay away from the tractor.

I was envious of the ease with which he came and went. 'We're only looking,' I said. 'Do you know what he's doing?'

As the swing seat arched towards us Jack jumped off and ran scornfully straight past, under the rowan tree and out of the side gate. We could hear the hollow clumping of his boots down the steps breaking out beneath us in the lane. Then we watched him hitch himself over the gate and skip down the field towards the barn, waving his arms and calling out.

The boy stopped in mid swing and looked around over his shoulder. I pulled Biddy down with me, tucking our heads onto our chests, holding her arm tightly. We could hear him saying something. I looked up. He was waving Jack back, shouting at him, 'Ha'way, It's not safe!'

Jack's voice was thin and high, 'Can I do it?'

'No! It's not safe. Stay there!'

'Can I watch?'

'Don't come any nearer.'

His voice was like a bass guitar.

'What's Jack doing?' Biddy asked

'Being a pain in the arse!' I said, irritated by the indignity of having to hide. Embarrassment was like a disease.

Daddy had always sneered at the Burdens, ever since we saw them going to chapel when the two boys used to wear jackets and matching shirts, like the Partridge family, Daddy said.

Now we were older, now that life at the cottage had become a fortress from which I could only peer through slits to the outside world, the presence of the boy became a tantalising gift. Like the smudge of a boat on the horizon, any boat; it offered the dream of a way out.

Mr Simnett told Mummy stories about them, about how Mr Burden's aunts had lived in our cottage until they were put in a home by the council; about the two boys, the one that died, who was only thirteen, the same age as Amelia is now, how the brakes of the tractor weren't working properly and somehow the whole thing had flipped over and fallen onto him in the yard; how the elder one had become a bit of a handful; how he was driving his father to distraction.

It didn't matter to me that nothing would happen. It was enough to have the glimmer of a possibility. In London, I didn't know any boys. We lived in a street where we never played out. 'Robert,' I tested the name. 'Robert Burden,' and for the moment put it top of a list that included Sherlock Holmes, Heathcliffe, Bob Dylan, Steve McQueen and (though I despised myself for it) John Travolta.

I watched him swing the great hammer round again and a surf of stone skitter off into the undergrowth. He had knots along his arms and round his neck. His skin glowed as if someone had burnished him all over with the back of a spoon. There was a fuzz of hair under his armpits like brush strokes and a solid board for his belly. He could lift you off your feet, I thought, like a baby. His arms would be iron, and his legs.

'Why isn't he wearing any clothes?'

'He is!'

'I can see his titties.'

'Shut up — he'll hear us!'

It was remarkable to me how even the sight of him could lift my lethargy, as if something in the light had positively changed, gazing through the eye of a needle to a creature that one day in one form or another I might reach out and touch.

Now, when I am sent out collecting wood or gooseberries, I feel as if he might be watching and it makes me hold myself properly. I make sure to run down a field as if I was born to it, not a foot out of place. And if I happen to trip, I buzz like an electric fire in case he might have seen. He is always alongside me and we'll embark on a whole new map of a world that will have nothing to do with anything in the past except to celebrate the coincidence of where our paths might have crossed — the jetty on the reservoir, the oak tree in the bottom field, the quarries, sledging on the lane.

And then that night I have the strangest dream. I dream it twice . . .

Daddy is at the top of the staircase, blocking out the light. The stairs are unbelievably narrow, so that as he goes down, his shoulders bump against the walls on either side. By the time he reaches the bottom, his limbs have filled out and he has become dark and broad. He turns round to look at me, peering up through the liquid shadow that has collected in the well of the stairs. Something drops from my hand, or my mouth, in sheer astonishment. He has the long hair and bare body of the boy on the barn and he half smiles up at me before rushing off into the night, slamming the door behind him.

7

At the cottage, we can go for weeks and not see anyone. Only the milkman, Mr Simnett, calls to make it feel as if we have any connection to the outside world at all. He comes on Mondays, Wednesdays, Fridays, but often before anyone is up. If he catches us, he likes to stop for a chat. Mummy is sometimes in the mood; other times she sends Biddy out with the money and leaves the empty bottles on the doorstep.

His name is Cyril and he's very easily encouraged. Mummy likes to think she has a knack of getting on with ordinary people: with shopkeepers, with farmers, with old ladies. Daddy can't do it. He hides. When he's buying petrol, he'll put his hand through the half-open window, awkwardly, to collect the change. 'Thanks, mate,' he says and we cringe, at the way he puts it on.

But Mummy prides herself on the time Cyril takes to chat. When he hears her at the door, he peers round from fiddling with the bottles at the back of his van and his face breaks into a smile. He has a tweed cap that he raises on his finger to her.

Mummy encourages him by laughing at his stories. He tells her of the goings on at Ashridge House at the top of the valley, bought by a religious sect who light fires and dance in the garden at night; of the long undiscovered death of the couple who lived in the house by the post box; of when our cottage used to be the shop and belonged to the old sisters who fought like cat and dog. He talks about the weather, about the date for the Ellersdale Show, about the shooting season . . .

'Seen them about?' he says, nodding downhill with the peak of his cap, towards the farm.

'We haven't really . . . not this time,' Mummy says with just a hint of wondering whether she should admit that we have so little to do with them and that she hasn't made more of an effort.

'She doesn't get out much, the missus that is, not since that lad of hers . . .'

'It must have been so dreadful . . . at the time. I still can't really believe it.'

'Do you know, there's at least three people in my lifetime have died on a farm. They're dangerous places with the machinery and that. But that family, they've had bad luck . . . You know about his brother I expect? Eddie, Graham Burden's brother?'

'I don't know anything about his family. I didn't know he had a brother.'

'He doesn't – not now.'

'What happened?'

Cyril looks round behind him along the road, and then adjusts his face, leaning in towards her, lowering his voice, 'He topped himself. One Christmas,' and then he adds hastily, seeing the incredulous expression on her face, 'It was years ago, twenty years or so.'

'What? You don't mean *killed himself*?'

Cyril is shaking his head. 'A long time ago now, just before Graham and her was married, it was. I thought you might have heard about it.'

'No. Not at all – God, how awful! What a horrid thing to live with! Did he do it there? At the farm?'

Cyril seems to expand with the luck of having such a great bait to reel her in with. 'He was in the old barn down the field, the tumbled one. Very sad, it was. I knew him, knew him quite well. If anything you'd have thought it 'ud be Graham – much more reserved like – but no, it was Eddie who hung himself. No one could have predicted it.'

Cyril's puffed-up with the shine of Mummy's interest. He loves to have her like that, listening to him, smiling down on him like he's important. She was a nice lady, he told them along the road: interested, caring.

His fingers are in the empty milk bottles like udders. They are contorted and fat, clinking together as he pulls the glass towards him. Thinking he's on his way, I come from behind the living-room door. Too soon. He spots me and hesitates, coughs, winking at Mummy for her to admire how he can handle the switch in tone, changing the subject: 'By, you've grown up since last year, haven't you? I bet you're leading lads a merry dance now, isn't she, Mother?'

I look down at my sandals.

'A shy one you've got there, Missus, give her a few years, eh?' He's like Benny Hill, I think, Ernie, the fastest milkman in the west. And he wears that white overall that makes him look like a milk bottle on legs.

'What did he say?' I follow her into the living room, where Daddy's bent over his desk.

She ignores me. 'You'll never guess what Cyril's just told me.'

Daddy glances up, then back at the string of letters along the ridge of his typewriter. He types with his two first fingers in bursts, lifting them now from the keys as if about to launch another attack.

She's still standing there, refusing to go on until she has his attention.

'He says that Mr Burden had a brother who killed himself at the farm.' She delivers it with the satisfaction of seeing his fingers drop.

Daddy strokes the hair back from his forehead. 'What – down the road?'

'Yes, he hung himself.'

'When?'

'Says it was twenty years ago, something like that – But think how terrible? *Twice!*'

'Not exactly twice. The boy didn't kill himself, did he? It was an accident.'

Mummy looks irritated. 'It's the same thing, pretty much, two deaths . . .'

Daddy sighs, still not willing to concede to her. 'I think you'll find that killing yourself is a bit different.' He turns away, something on the 'w' of the typewriter seeming to catch his eye, and he strokes it with the tip of his finger, then throws out, underarm, 'And there's a difference again, isn't there, between the people who say they're going to do it and those who actually pull it off – quite a big difference!'

'Is that supposed to be a dig at me?'

'Not particularly.'

Her eyes are flashing but she makes a supreme effort to contain herself and says pointedly, 'All I can say is that it puts things into perspective, doesn't it? It makes me see how lucky we are – the children all healthy; we're still together, aren't we? It makes everything seem rather trivial by comparison.'

He hunches up and looks sideways at me. 'All right, Ruth? Coffee?'

Mummy won't let it go; 'It makes me think we're well off, doesn't it you?'

I told Amelia but not Biddy or Jack; I told her as if it had happened yesterday and she was satisfyingly astounded. 'God! How did he do it?'

Hearing the story about the man who killed himself made us re-examine the other boy's death too. I found myself looking at the farm in a different way, as if it was an intriguingly blighted place like Wuthering Heights. And I made a point of shutting up the others if I caught them singing too loudly in the garden.

I didn't know anyone who'd ever killed themselves, although, when they sang they hoped they'd die before they got old, I thought I knew exactly what they meant. There was something admirable about it, courageous: having the courage of your convictions. There were girls at school who didn't eat for days and I kicked myself because I couldn't even starve myself for a morning to make a point.

The other thing was that it made me begin to realise about other people's lives. Before that, the Burdens were just a given when we came to the cottage – part of the furniture, like the schoolhouse, the trees in the graveyard, the river. I tried to recall how it felt when we first heard about the accident. I don't remember it making much of a difference to us. It was like a branch had come off a tree: unless you'd known about it, you'd not really have noticed. There wasn't a weeping or a wailing coming from the place, just a quietness, maybe more of a keeping themselves to themselves. Now though, because it touched Robert, because I'd let him into my dreams, I found everything about the Burdens, any crumb of new information, infinitely fascinating.

It's Jack who has most to do with them, so-called *helping* Mr

Burden. Most days this summer he goes off first thing and often doesn't come back until the evening, stinking of cow dung, acting like nothing has ever happened down there.

Mummy brought it up with Daddy again, waving it about like a flag as if it could make whatever was going on between them shrink in comparison. But Daddy refused to be drawn. He said that probably every house for miles had its own suicide somewhere along the line; that if he'd been brought up on a clapped-out farm at the bottom of a valley, he might have been tempted to do the same.

'How can you say that? You always say you love it here.'

'Maybe it's a question of having the choice—'

'You've changed your tune!'

8

C yril was the last person from outside to see me for days. I couldn't risk bumping into anyone with three burgeoning spots on my chin, presage of the inevitable, which I dreaded every time as if for the first time. It had been brewing for days and now it had arrived I couldn't think of anything else, keeping in, keeping still, sure the dogs from miles around would sniff me out.

The cottage is the worst place and it has to happen at least once during the summer, sometimes twice. It's almost impossible to keep secret. If Mummy knows, she makes a fuss and buys bumper packs of sanitary towels, waving them about like a football rattle in the chemist's.

Not telling her, there's no way of buying the pads and there's times I've had to make do with cotton wool and holly and ivy Sellotape from the cupboard. I hide the knickers in a pocket of the suitcase. I keep the disgusting evidence in a plastic bag under the pile of newspapers in our room. Only when there's no one around can I get rid of it.

The dump is just outside Ellershead in an old quarry. There's a council KEEP OUT sign on the gate. A few years ago we used to go there quite often looking for treasure. Daddy picked up china souvenirs of Haltwhistle and Penrith and, almost full size, an old shop dummy on a pedastal advertising Pears soap, naked and pale-skinned, with a miniscule waist, arms above her head like a ballerina. He put her in the kitchen at first, but she ended up in the cellar because Mummy said she didn't like to feel watched when she was cooking.

We stopped coming in the end when someone driving past shouted over that they'd report us and that it wasn't the place any decent person would take their kids.

Today, because they've all gone to Alston again to do the washing, I have slunk out on the bike with the package of bloody pads stashed in the zipped-up saddlebag. The ride is uphill and a struggle. I have to walk the last bit of it, up the track, laying the bike on the verge by the gate, all the time alert to the possibility of someone watching.

When I lift out the bag it feels as if it contains something living; the plastic is soft and warm. Quickly I half swing, half hurl it over the gate as far as I can. But it falls way short of my aim and I look around anxiously, wondering whether I should climb the gate and chuck it further in. At the same time, out of habit, I can't help scouring for booty, disentangling rubber tyres, toys, rusty springs, half a sofa, bedheads, sinks, dazzled by the choice until the objects begin to dance before my eyes, alive with the suggestion of a snout or a tail, the twitch of an ear. I ride back with my skin crawling, pumping at the pedals of the bicycle to get away.

Then I spend the afternoon sunk on my bed groaning like the wolf with stones sewn in her stomach. I can't read, I can't even listen to my tapes. When they get back there is an irritating clatter of excitement through the door. Biddy bursts into the bedroom. 'Guess what!'

I don't even look up.

'You'll never guess!'

'What?'

'Daddy's brought a telly!'

'*Bought?*' I say but raise myself on the bed. That was almost the first rule about the cottage: no telly. And it was the hardest fought. Every holiday a litany of the programmes we would be missing, how we'd die if we weren't able to keep up.

'Where is it?'

'They're bringing it in when all the shopping's unpacked.'

I can hear bags being carried, buffing against the stairway and Amelia complaining that Jack never has to help. Mummy is downstairs clattering – bread in the bread bin, bags of potatoes, apples, the open and shut kiss of the fridge.

I appear at the living-room door. 'Biddy says you've bought a telly.'

'Do you think we should we take it back?' Daddy asks.

'I thought we weren't allowed telly here.'

'Well, it's all the same to me. I'm quite happy to take it back.'

'No! We want it! Ruth doesn't have to watch it!'

'I didn't say I didn't want it, just that it seems a bit funny if we weren't allowed before.'

'Don't be such an old maid,' he says.

It took two hours to determine that the only place the aerial worked was hanging out of the window, and then, ideally, someone had to be standing on the seat with their arm out of the window at a particular angle. It was a small black and white portable, but to Jack and Biddy, to all of us, it was the Ritz. Because it was raining, Daddy relented and let us watch the end of an old Audrey Hepburn film. She had such beautiful clothes and I felt like a lump watching her, wanting to be her, living in a world of music and parties and being fallen in love with and ending up with the right man, thank God, getting out of the taxi and finding the kitten in the rain and the man and falling into his arms, knowing he'd be there for ever. 'Ruth's crying,' Amelia sneered.

'I'm not! Piss off!'

'You are,' said Biddy. 'I can see your eyes. I wish we had a kitten.'

Thursday is *Top of the Pops* night, and it's agreed that if we eat all our supper and come down straight after it's finished to do the washing-up, then we're allowed to watch it. Daddy comes with us and sits with a catalogue open on his knee.

Mummy doesn't like pop music and stays downstairs listening to *The Archers*, which she never misses. But we've hardly worked out where we're all sitting when we hear the violent grating of a chair and a pounding on the stairs. Mummy breaks into the living room with something held out in her hand.

'How do you explain this?'

We look up only momentarily distracted from the titles. Daddy doesn't say a word.

'Well? Do I need to ask who it is?' She holds out a glossy square photograph and jabs at it with the other hand.

Daddy sighs, folds his arms, but looks straight at the TV and after a detectable hesitation says, 'I've had it in my wallet so that I remember to give it to her when I see her.'

'Why've you got a photo of her there in the first place?'

'It's from that exhibition, the opening – someone gave it to me. I said I'd pass it on.'

'Really! Do you think I'm a fool? Go on. Why don't you tell them the truth for once? What are you doing with a photograph of her in your wallet?'

Daddy laughs weakly, derisively and shrugs.

Mummy is practically dancing. 'Go on. Tell us!'

We're irritated now. Why does she have to choose our favourite programme? We refuse to look round, watching her hopping-mad performance out of the corners of our eyes. Why does she have to make trouble? Why does she try so hard to find things out?

'You must think I'm so stupid. How dare you? How dare you bring this into my house? In front of your children! How the fuck can you do it?'

Daddy shrugs again with his hands as if to deny all knowledge.

And we believe him. We really do. Although we're still trying to listen to the rundown so that we can be the first to pronounce 'fine' or 'crap' as each song is flagged up.

At Number 30 It's Joe Jackson wondering 'Is She Really Going Out with Him?' ('Fine!')

At Number 29, still hanging on in there, Showaddywaddy, with 'Sweet Little Rock N' Roller' (simultaneously Amelia shouts out 'fine!' and I shout 'crap!'; Biddy and Jack follow like echoes, 'fine', 'crap'.)

At Number 28 . . .

'I've had enough! I've absolutely had enough. None of you care. None of you gives a shit. I might as well kill myself. None of you would care.' She opens the door, slams it shut in her wake and we hear her rattle down the stairs, pause at the bottom and then hurtle back up like she always does, never leaving it alone, crashing back through the door.

'How on earth can you do this to me? After all the years I've worked myself to the bone for you. I've typed for you, cleaned for you, skivvied for you, painted, plastered, killed myself for you – for this! How dare you?' She turns again on her heel crying as she goes down the stairs, 'I'll kill myself. I will . . .' We hear the pantry slam in the kitchen and a tiny mouse lock click on the door. And then the biscuit tin, where the headache pills and plasters are kept, opening like a cymbal.

Daddy sits quite still. 'Leave her. She'll be all right.'

None of us move. We hear from underground, 'I'm taking pills!'

It's been four weeks and number one is still the Boomtown Rats, 'I don't like Mondays', which is a great relief to us all as otherwise it would have been Cliff Richard, *crap!* Amelia, Biddy and Jack all begin singing along. I won't sing in front of anyone else.

Suddenly, the door of the pantry is kicked open and she screams into the kitchen, right below us. 'Are you satisfied now! Are you happy! Why don't you just go to her! Leave us in peace!'

Daddy raises his eyes and chews his lip. 'She'll calm down,' he says, 'she'll be all right.'

When we go downstairs to do the washing-up, we can hear her crying in the pantry, talking to herself.

'Shall I make some coffee, Mummy?' I ask loudly.

There's no answer.

'We're doing the washing-up . . .'

Neither of us feel we can go in there so we make a show of clearing the table, stacking plates, filling the bowl from the kettle. After a bit, it's as if she isn't even there, Amelia starts singing, 'My mamma told me-e-e if I was goode-e-e, that she would buy me-e-e a rubber dolle-e-e.' She takes a breath and I turn towards her, 'Shut up!', motioning towards the pantry door.

'Make me!'

'Just shut up!'

'My sister told he-e-e-r . . .' She is right at my ear, 'I kissed a soldie-e-e-r . . .'

'Piss off!' I pick out the dishcloth and flick her with it.

She grabs the cloth from my hand, dips it back in the sink and screws it into my face, all over my hair. I shriek in disbelief, rooted to the spot.

Suddenly Mummy is in the room, blazing at us, 'What's going on?'

I am dripping, stinking of cabbage water. 'Her!'

'I didn't do anything!'

'Mad cow!'

Mummy opens her mouth like a red sore. She screams into the room so that it lands on everything, shaking the mirror, 'Shut up, both of you, just shut the fuck up. I've had enough!'

Daddy thuds across the floor above our heads. 'Bed! All of you! Now! This instant! No arguing!'

So we're lying here, bundled up and it's not even dark. Amelia whispers cold bloodedly, 'Daddy looks like he's going to have a nervous breakdown.'

'So does Mummy,' I say. 'Happy families!'

'What's a nervous breakdown?' Biddy asks, rolling round in her sleeping bag.

'Talking to yourself. Going all googly eyes.'

'Why are they like it?'

'Who knows?'

'Do you remember the Orkneys?' Amelia says to me, and she offers it like an apology, an invitation.

The Orkneys was the one holiday we'd had away from Northumberland and I know exactly what she means by it, spluttering in acknowledgement.

'What? Tell me,' Biddy protests.

'Shush!'

Biddy and Jack had been babies that holiday. They hadn't and wouldn't get it.

'What are you *incinerating*?' Amelia is up on her elbow, laughing over the top of Biddy's head, mimicking her to further cement our temporary alliance.

We'd been lent a bothy that belonged to a great uncle of ours and we were sleeping all together in bunk beds in a room that, like the other two rooms, had a scallop shell full of rat poison in it, just by the door. It was our first night and we were so excited, by the sea crossing, by being in a different place, we couldn't sleep. It stayed light until very late and we whispered to each other to keep ourselves awake until even Mummy and Daddy shut themselves in their bedroom next door for the night. After five minutes or so, I heard an insistent creaking sound. 'Did you hear that? Just then?'

'What?' Amelia was at a right angle to me, already alert and apprehensive.

There were wooden batons running along the wall all the way round the room just wide enough for a creature to scuttle along. On each of the top bunks, which the two of us had appropriated, the baton ran just by our heads. There it was again! We both cried as loud as we dared, 'Daddy! Mummy! There're rats in our room!'

Daddy appeared after a bit, naked but dark against the pearly light of the doorway.

'What is it?' he hissed. 'It's time you were asleep. Don't wake the babies.'

'We can hear rats. They're in our room. We heard them.'

He was breathing heavily but he cocked his ear to the ceiling for a minute to humour us. There was nothing, just the steady sucking of a thumb, like an engine ticking away somewhere.

'Go to sleep. There's nothing. Don't be so silly, just go to sleep.'

He dropped the latch on the door and went back to their room. But five minutes later it was there again, a regular squeaking in the wood, *ee-ee-ee*. Everything happened exactly the same, like a repeat in music: calling for them, Daddy coming in, not bothering to listen this time, shutting us up more angrily and closing the door on us.

But then – we couldn't believe it! – it happened again. This time we waited until we were sure, completely sure, before insisting, both of us together, that they hadn't gone away. But he refused to come in. He bellowed at us from their bed, 'Belt up! Belt up! If you dare wake the babies . . . !'

The sound didn't come back after that.

It was only recently that it had dawned on me. I was telling the story at school, a story about rats, when it occurred to me, as it occurred to the girls I was telling, that it was something entirely different. I had broken it to Amelia when I got home from school, 'Oh my God!' She'd giggled incredulously through her fingers. 'God!'

'Tell me,' said Biddy, 'tell me! What is it?'

'Nothing. Just that time when we thought there were rats, you won't remember.'

'Yes, I do.'

'You were too young.'

'I do remember.'

'Maybe we'll hear them again?' Amelia says.

'But there aren't any rats,' Biddy pleads, 'are there?'

9

When Daddy is writing none of us is allowed near. We have to keep quiet and out of the way. He works in the living room, the room with the fire, where the two of them sleep at night on a big mattress in the corner. He is writing today with the door firmly shut. He's shrieking and banging and whistling. 'Jesus Christ almighty – come on!!' The typewriter is a battery of gunfire. The silences are alive. I knock, with a cup of coffee. There's an animal grunt as I open the door and find him sitting up on his haunches on the swivel chair, hands raking through the hair over his ears, with a sound escaping like a kettle.

'I've brought you coffee.'

'Put it there . . . thanks.'

I place the cup on an old pile of pink and yellow copy paper. I hesitate because he doesn't go straight back to the typing but breathes out and looks at me offhand, conspiratorially.

'God, your mother's mad – What do *you* think I should do?'

I laugh, like he does, through my nose. 'I don't know.'

'You can see how difficult it is, can't you? She's making it impossible.'

When I don't say anything, he adds, 'Maybe I should leave for a bit, find somewhere else to live . . . until things calm down.'

'I don't know . . . maybe you should.'

I go out after that, towards the track, not sure where I'm heading. I can't get the way he looked at me out of my head – as if he trusts me to make the decision, as if I am party to the decision and I've already helped make it by agreeing with him or not disagreeing. It's something I've only recently become aware of: the two halves of them inside me, battling it out – one side him, and the other her – so distinct sometimes that you could cut a line down the middle of me.

I climb the series of gates that lead from grassland and thistles to the scrub and heather of the high moor. Whatever the weather, there is always the tug of a wind up here and birds hovering overhead, asserting to any creature listening that the planet belongs to them, the language for it exclusively theirs. Sometimes the wind is so bad that it is only the telegraph poles that seem to keep the land from taking off all together.

There are adders on the moor and you have to be wary of wading through the heather. I climb, following the sheep tracks high enough so I can just see beyond our own valley into the hazy distance of the next. It's as far as I ever come and when I get to a clear patch of ground by the old sheepfold, I chuck down my sweater and collapse flat out tuning in, as my own breathing subsides, to the persistent hum of foraging bees. Under my back the whole warm world is turning. It's like being part of a gigantic clock, the earth grinding on its cogs, circulating in a million different combinations of going round.

The sun engraves red to my closed eyelids as if everything outside is on fire. Like a nuclear war. Like being the very last person alive. We've agreed it at school: if they dropped the bomb, you'd have to grab a boy. It's fine to die before you get old, but you couldn't die without having a boy. Robert. Robbie. Rob. All the iron filings in my blood yearn towards the bottom of the valley, where he might be, the deep emerald burn of the valley . . .

Suddenly, I'm aware of a buffeting, something more bodily than air around me. I squint through half-opened eyes to see looming above me a great moulting, snuffling creature. I leap to my feet, clumsily lifting my arms at what is now a gang of them stumbling towards me. They hesitate only slightly and then pack in tighter around me, not remotely scared, nudging each other on. I make a ridiculous sheep sound, but to no effect; they jostle together, breathing heavily, pointing at me their hard black eyes.

Whoever else might be looking I retreat, not daring to turn my back on them until, in an ungainly panic, I climb the gate and retrace my steps, humiliated, booed from the moor all the way back to the cottage.

'Where have you been? Is Biddy with you?' Mummy is lying in wait for me by the front door, looking haggard and jumpy. 'Have you seen Biddy?'

'No.'

'Do you know where she is?'

'No. I've been up the track.'

'Did she follow you?'

'I don't think so – no'

'We thought she might be with you . . .'

'No.'

'Oh God! Biddy! Biddy! Biddy!' Mummy is halfway down the stairs and shouting out from the back door across the garden. Amelia's on the swing. 'Maybe she's gone down to the river?'

'On her own?' Mummy asks sharply, accusingly.

'She might have—'

'What do you mean?' She's looking round at me and immediately I feel the dead hand of responsibility.

'She likes the river . . .'

Mummy looks withering and sweeps out of the garden shouting, 'Biddy!' all along the path like a dog's name.

I follow her reluctantly. Amelia stays behind, stationary on the swing.

'You shouldn't have left her on her own.'

'I thought she was with Amelia.'

'Biddy! Biddy!'

The sun is in and out of cloud, watching our progress. When it's out, it's hard to think that anything can be wrong; when it hides, I can see a pool of floating hair, the coathanger of Biddy's skinny shoulder blades. In no time Mummy reaches the stile and I can see Mr Burden looking up at us from the farmyard, hesitating to climb onto his tractor.

'You haven't seen Biddy down here, have you?' Mummy shouts across.

Mr Burden seems to consider it before answering, screwing up his mouth, 'Not that I'm aware of—'

'If you see her . . . ?'

'I'll send her straight on home.'

'Thanks.' She's hitched up her skirt to go over the stile and is already searching along the bank of the river, like the keenest bird watcher. 'Biddy!' adding under her breath, 'I can't believe you'd let her go on her own.'

'She's been before. She's been on her own before.'

Mummy ignores me. 'You haven't seen her since breakfast, is that right?'

It was a question addressed to the river; I mutter, 'Yes, I think so.'

'We'll have to go to the police – she's not down here – Biddy!'

I believe her. This is going to turn out to be the end of the story. The summer Biddy died, the summer that would be with us all for ever, indelible. And everyone I ever meet will have to coax it out of me and we'll have to book a plot in the graveyard, and a dome . . .

The hands!

The thought slips into my head as easy as a knife and there's blood everywhere. The hands. If she's dead, it's my fault. She'll be buried in me and I will carry her for the rest of my life, like a splinter. I hate her if she's died. I hate her for dying because of me.

'John, John!' Mummy's breathless from the climb up the hill. 'John, we can't find her!'

'What is it?' Daddy sounds tetchy, leaning out of the living-room door to see what's wrong.

Mummy stands at the bottom of the stairs looking up at him. She hammers every word home, 'We can't find her. I've looked every-where. I've been down to the river, asked at the farm, she's nowhere to be seen.'

'Calm down. She must be somewhere.'

'She's not here!' Mummy flares like a blowtorch. 'I *knew* she would get upset by all this. I told you she would get upset. I'm going to the police. Are you coming?'

Daddy sighs. 'Are you sure you've looked?' He doesn't expect a reply and as she shoulders past him at the top of the stairs he bows and follows in her wake, out of the front door, pulling the car keys from his pocket.

We all get in. As if she couldn't risk losing anyone else, Mummy pushes Jack in next to me so I'm forced against Amelia, who's snivelling by now. Then she hands herself back around the car, folding into the front seat and slamming the door so that the wing mirror droops. Daddy tries to start the engine, once, twice. He puts the car in gear. 'Come on you bastard!' and checks in his mirror, pulling the wheel to the right with both hands.

Then he stops. His shoulders drop.

'What are you doing? Come on, what are you doing?'

He doesn't say a word but breathes out, shaking his head slightly.

'John, I'll drive! Come on!' Mummy's practically screaming at him.

'Look behind you,' Daddy says wearily.

Before we turn round we can hear, 'Wait! Wait for me! – Wait!' She's holding a doll by its arm. 'Wait!'

Mummy opens the car door and swings out her legs. 'Where have you been?' Her voice is dry and deathly.

'Nowhere.'

She begins quietly but builds to a pitch of exasperation, 'Where have you been? We've looked absolutely everywhere. We've been shouting all over the place. You must have heard.'

'No.' Biddy's looking down at her feet, swinging the doll.

'Where were you?'

'I was asleep, in the stable.'

Jack and Amelia are out of the car. 'Can I go now?' Jack is twisting his back on them.

'I told you.' Amelia, still sulking, 'I told you she was all right.'

'Shut up.' Mummy says between her teeth and Amelia stomps off shouting back, 'You wouldn't care if it was me that was lost.'

It's hard after that to get the idea of a funeral out of my head, or the notion that somehow I was to blame. It's like the stink of fish, it stays around for days. There's something about Biddy that seems different. She looks younger, as though someone has subtracted the last two years from her and she's carrying Arabella, who she used to take everywhere, but who she'd lost interest in ages ago, left face-down in one of the old cots. Now Biddy is fussing over her again, doing up the buttons on her dresses, insisting, 'I didn't hear.'

'I don't believe you.'

'I didn't. Only the car. I thought you was going home without me.'

'You never do that again, do you hear – never!'

'But I didn't do nothing . . .'

'Never!'

'Ow! You're hurting!'

'Do you understand?'

'You're hurting me, Mummy!'

10

When she got Biddy back, Mummy didn't let her out of her sight. I think she always saw Biddy as her most stealable daughter, the most biddable. So she spent time in the morning brushing her hair, telling her she needed to count to one hundred to make it shine, making two plaits behind her ears. She dreamt up reasons to keep her at the kitchen table, painting flowers with her, making biscuits or patiently recounting the old stories in a way she'd long ago refused to do for us.

'Tell the time when you and Daddy met.'

'When I hid under the bed?'

'Yes, and the man was there . . .'

'Well, I went to see him, Daddy, when he was at university, and girls weren't really allowed in those days, and I had to hide under his bed when the old man came in to clean his room.'

'And you could just see his socks . . .'

'They were sort of purplish socks and polished shoes, and I was hiding so hard that I almost forgot to breathe.'

'Did he find you?'

'No, thank goodness, otherwise your dad would have got chucked out and I'd have been even more in the black books.'

'And then you got married.'

'Yes — we got married.'

'Did lots of people come?'

'No. Not lots. Just Granny and Grandpa and your other granny, and Daddy's sister.'

'Did you have bridesmaids?'

'No.'

'Did you have a long dress?'

'No – you've seen it in the photograph, it was short and grey.'

'Why didn't you have a nice dress?'

'I don't know – it wasn't the fashion.'

'I'm going to have a princess dress when I get married with puffy sleeves – and three bridesmaids.'

'I could have had you, couldn't I, if you'd have been born – you'd make such a lovely bridesmaid.'

'Where did you live in the olden days?'

'In a basement – right at the bottom of a house, underground almost – down lots of stairs. In Newcastle. That was when we had Ruth and I used to put her up on the windowsill and she'd watch all the footsteps coming to and fro, going to work, and she'd be as good as gold.'

'Was I really?' I wanted her to linger on the image of me as her child, before all the others, and make her remember again how good I'd been. Before the time when I was three or four and confided in her that I hated Amelia, thinking she might just send her back or away, but instead she had turned on me and said, if I really hated Amelia and if I told her anything like that again, I'd have to leave the house and go and live somewhere else.

'Hard to imagine it now, isn't it?'

'She was fat, though, wasn't she, and huge, and she didn't have any hair – She was the ugliest baby ever!'

'No, she wasn't. She was a perfectly sweet baby.'

'And when Amelia was born you thought you were having a big poo and when she came out, she came out in the bog!'

'It wasn't like that!'

'Ruth says that's what happened.'

'She's being silly.'

'What does it feel like – having a baby?'

'Well, I don't know really . . . Like falling over – hurting your knee.'

'Did you cry?'

'No, not really.'

'Then it was me.'

'Yes, and then we lived in Ilford Road, by the railway – Do you remember?'

'Was I pretty?'

'Of course you were. You were absolutely gorgeous. And then we all moved to London – and then we had Jack.'

'Why don't we stay here?'

'You know why – Because Daddy's got to work and his work's in London.'

'Why can't he work here? He does typing here.'

'There's things he needs to see in London, people.'

'*We* could live here.'

'Without Daddy?'

'We could live at Mrs Brown's. You said we could. Daddy could come and stay . . .'

'It might be boring, all the time – What about school?'

'It wouldn't.'

'You don't know that.'

'I do . . . So does it mean that I'm a Geordie, same as Ruth and Amelia?'

'I suppose so. You're Geordies, Jack's a cockney.'

'She doesn't sound like a Geordie.' I couldn't resist butting in. 'Go on, Biddy, say "thirty-three feathers – thinking they were flying home."'

'Firty-free-fevvers . . . on . . . finking – what did you say?'

'They were flying home.'

'"Flying home." See, I can.'

'Not exactly Geordie.'

' Say deodorant,' Amelia said to her, nudging me with her elbow.

'Devovovant.'

Both of us cackled with laughter. 'Where did you say you came from, Biddy? Disneyland?'

'Leave her alone, Ruth, just leave her alone! Biddy, do you want to come out with me for a walk? Let's get some fresh air, shall we?'

We could hear them through the window as they wound their way along the outside of the house, Biddy asking in her new lispy voice, 'Mummy, do you fink Mrs Burden's pretty?'

'Mrs Burden? Yes, she's quite pretty . . .'

'I fink she is.'

'Prettier than me?'

'She's got nice eyes.'

'Prettier than mine?'

'And nice teef.'

'Has she?

When Mummy and Biddy got back they brought out the tray, with KitKats arranged on a plate like a flower, laying it down on top of the low wall with a flourish. 'Shall we tell them, Biddy?'

Biddy was moving from one foot to the other coyly as if she'd been asked to perform to old ladies. 'What?' Amelia was surly, sensing that it might be yet another treat denied her.

'We bumped into Mr Burden, didn't we, on our walk, coming through the farmyard. And . . .' Mummy looked around, and although she had our attention, it was Daddy's eyes – fixed since she'd appeared to the insides of his paper – she was trying to reach. 'And,' she continued emphatically, 'he's asked us all if we'd like to help with the haymaking.'

Daddy looked up then and pulled the paper towards him. 'What? *Asked?* I've hardly heard him speak, let alone *ask* anything.'

'Well, he did, didn't he Biddy? Pretty much . . .' and then she added more stridently, 'It's what people do in the countryside, help each other out. Don't you think it would be a nice gesture – break the ice? Especially after what happened.'

'Don't *you* think,' he replied, 'that it's a bit late for that – a bit late in the day . . .'

'It's never too late,' she said, fixing him with a brittle smile. 'After all, we don't want to be *tourists* do we? Don't we want to be a *part* of something?' She said it as if she were quoting from somebody else, from him perhaps. But then she lost her nerve and her voice became high and flat, 'Anyhow, I said we'd be very pleased to. I said we'd go down there tomorrow, if it's still dry.'

'Things have changed since *Tess of the d'Urbervilles*,' Daddy muttered, opening up his paper. In a sudden fury she snatched it from him.

'It's *exactly* what people do down here in the country, and it's the least we can do, don't you think?'

'OK, OK . . .'

'I feel dreadful that we come here – we've been coming for years – and we don't even know them. We must have been the last to know when that accident happened. It's embarrassing. It shouldn't be like that. Not in a small place like this. We should be making more of an effort. And, anyway, it might stop the children bickering – I'm sick of them bickering with each other – it'll give them something worthwhile to do. And it can work both ways: if we help them now, if we're friendly, maybe one day they'll help us out.'

'With what?' he snorted.

'Don't keep saying that – *with what?*'

'Do we have to?' Amelia whined.

Mummy jumped on her. 'You don't know what you're talking about! It's a perfectly nice thing to do, and it'll be fun, actually! We're all going. I said we would. We're all going for once and that's the end of it.'

I didn't say a word. I'd already decided I would wear my cords, the ones I'd taken in. They were the colour of hay. I went to bed early. Robert. I tried to imagine him – I had no clear impression of his face. For the time being I pictured him as a combination of Marlon Brando, the wild one, who I'd cut out on his motorbike and stuck in a scrapbook, looking out, rebellious, and – I slipped him in – John Travolta. It was one or other version creeping up behind me, arms around me, breath in my ear. Biddy was still awake.

'Stop making noises.'

'I'm breathing.'

'You're making funny noises.'

'Piss off!'

'You are! I'm going to tell—'

'I'm only breathing.'

'You're snorting.'

'I'm asleep.'

I buried my head in my sleeping bag resisting the temptation to kick out at her, keen to reassemble my dream – on the back of a motorbike, my cheek against the cold leather of his back, the zip of the sleeping bag on my cheek like the zip of his jacket or the zip of the bike wheel tearing up the hill.

When Amelia came in I could hear Biddy whispering to her and sniggering. *How the worm turns!* Then they bellowed in stereo, 'Dad-dy. Will you turn the light out.'

The bike stood dead upright, balancing on the tail-end of its momentum.

'Dad-dy, will you turn the light out?'

'Turn it out yourselves!'

'Dad-dy, will you turn the light out?'

I could hear his footsteps thumping across the floorboards in the other room and the latch lifting, his hand fumbling for the switch. 'Belt up, you lazy bitches! Good night!' The light was gone, the door slammed shut.

Amelia began to giggle again and Biddy joined in. I could hear them stuffing their mouths with their sleeping bags. 'Shut up!'

There was a precarious stillness and then Biddy, in a small high-pitched voice, squirmed in her bag, piping, 'Oh, darling!'

Amelia was killing herself laughing.

'Oh, Robbie, darling, don't stop!'

'What are you on about?' I could only sound feeble in the face of their combined attack.

'No, don't stop, please don't stop.' Biddy minced and wriggled in her bag.

The haymaking morning took for ever to arrive and I lay, it seemed for hours, in the disintegrating greyness of the room forbidding myself to be the first to make a move. Finally, Mummy came in and pulled down the sheet from the window. 'It's a beautiful day,' she said, her knuckles face down on the ledge, rocking forwards on the hinges of her wrists, staring out across the valley, 'just beautiful!'

I pretended to wake up. The others were stirring and groaning.

'Jack wears his clothes in bed,' Biddy announced. 'He does it on school days too!'

'Don't tell tales; I'm not interested.'

'But he stinks!' Biddy persisted. 'It's not fair.'

Mummy ignored her. 'Come on, up you get, or we'll be late. We mustn't let them down.'

My heart was racing. I set off downstairs for a wash, filling the enamel bowl from the kettle. I was in my vest, leaning over splashing handfuls of water under my arms. The flannel was lying in a heap on the side, smelling of onion. It hadn't been used by any of us for over a week I splashed again and then rubbed with the very edge of the towel and went upstairs to get dressed.

Amelia was pulling on a skirt.

'What are you putting that on for?'

'None of your business.'

'You can't wear a skirt. We're working – it's not Sunday school – they'll think you're mad.'

'I can wear what I like.'

'You'll show us up.'

'Don't care.'

'Why don't you wear jeans like any normal person?'

'It's not up to you, what I wear.'

'Well, ask Mummy, then.'

Everything I said bounced off her. I could smell the warm, sickly poppies and feel the electricity of the frizz in her hair, like nylon carpet.

'Stupid cow.'

'Cows eat grass, grass is nature, nature is beautiful . . .'

I slammed the door behind me. It bounced out of its latch, open again, like her face, and I hurled myself down the stairs to get away from her.

Mummy was peering at the grill; there was a smell of burnt toast. She surfaced, and turned round. 'I'm so looking forward to this.'

Daddy cleared his throat. 'Lizzie, I've got a lot on . . .'

For a moment her face clouded. 'I've promised we'd all be there – even for a bit.'

'I'll have to see how it goes – I've got to be back by lunchtime, at the latest.'

'That's all I'm asking. Just show your face, show them you're willing.'

I could hardly eat. My mouth was dry and the porridge turned in it like cement.

'It'll be so good for the children, don't you think, learning how it all works?'

Daddy grunted grudgingly. 'Fine.'

I could hear Amelia and Biddy coming out onto the stairs, clutching each other like Donny and Marie, singing 'Puppy Love'.

Our boots on the tarmac of the road sounded like hooves. Mummy was ahead, swinging her arms, her hair tied back in a ponytail, her skin peachy. If only I'd inherited that skin! I still had a spot, undisguisable, on my chin and two or three waiting for the slightest breeze to expose them under my fringe. I was worried that the smell of TCP might linger about me. My fringe was long and I'd held it, like I did most nights, with a snake belt to keep the two horns of hair from curling up. It was flattened now to a thick ridge across my forehead. I could feel the elastic press of the belt where it had circled my head so definitely that in a sudden flash of horror I grabbed to check it wasn't still in place.

There was already activity in the farmyard and my heart skipped as I recognised Robert with his shirt, only half buttoned, hanging loose from his trousers, unloading from the back of the trailer and taking stuff into the barn. Mr Burden, in his dark blue overalls, appeared from the door. He looked up towards the racket of boots, putting his fist to his forehead as if he was dazzled by sun and nodded hello. Mummy ran the last bit of the way, hurrying into the yard. 'I do hope we're not late?'

Mr Burden had crooked teeth, too many for his mouth. Very occasionally his smile broke out like a hard nut cracked. If he had to say something he looked just to the left or the right of you, or down or up at the sky, but never at you.

'No hurry, Mr . . .?' he said, nodding at Daddy.

'It's John. Lizzie and John, please.'

Mr Burden nodded again.

'Jack's down here already, isn't he? We don't see much of him these days – I hope he's not a nuisance to you.'

'Not at all. Good little helper. Rob?'

Robert came round and stood next to him, taller by half a head, his dark hair falling in a long fringe over the side of his face. I couldn't look at him.

'Hello, darling.' Mummy held out her arms to Jack who was following behind Robert like his shadow; he shrank back.

Amelia smirked, mouthing, '*Darling!*'

Mr Burden looked at a loss. 'Well, now, shall we get going? Are we all set?' He turned to Mummy. 'Do you want to come up with us on the trailer?'

'Oh!' She clapped her hands, as if it were the biggest treat, and he moved forwards with her, unsure of himself, taking her elbow almost as if he was asking her to dance. He had thick nails cut very short so that the skin grew in a bulge around them – strong stubby fingers.

She had her arms raised slightly as if to say she'd done it all before, she could perfectly manage. She pressed her palms to the bottom of the trailer and hoisted herself up, wincing but laughing as she caught her knee. She knelt up, shuffling forward on the boards and brushing herself down. 'There we are! Come on then! If I can do it . . . up you come!'

Robert was last, but seemed to decide against getting up with us. He slouched round to where Mr Burden was sitting waiting in the cab and climbed onto the step holding the frame, leaning out from him, looking straight ahead. Mr Burden reached down, turned something at his knees and shook the gear stick. The whole contraption shuddered, then spluttered into life with an explosion of noise. As we began to move Jack and Biddy sprawled and shouted out in excitement, grabbing on as the tractor gave a further jolt forwards and lumbered noisily out of the farmyard. Mr Burden was steering with one hand; he turned his head briefly and with a glance seemed to take us all in. He was like the man who worked the roundabout at Brockwell Park, weaving in and out of the horses, immune to the excitement and the up and down and round and round, deaf to the din, pocketing the money and indifferent to the whole lot of us.

11

The hay dust stuck to our lips like sugar. By midday the stubble had hardened in the sun to a bed of nails. Biddy's arms and face were scarlet and she had been sent to sit against the wall, out of the glare, but Mummy, Amelia and I were each determined to prove ourselves, wearily raking loose strands of cut hay back into line.

Robert's shirt was round his waist. He was way down the field pitching bales up to his father on the trailer. Daddy had gone home after an hour. It had been embarrassing watching him trying to lift the stacks, straining every vein in his head and neck. He had been puce with the effort, and had yellow wheals across his palms from the baler cord. Even Mummy thought he should stop and was relieved when he said he had a headache, work to do, and, sorry, he'd have to get off home.

Every now and again a rabbit would appear from nowhere, running lopsidedly along the ridge of the field, delirious, disoriented, looking as if it felt the sight of a gun trained behind its ears. Crows circled and landed despondently further off like bits of black bin liner.

Mummy leant against her wooden rake, wiping her forehead with the back of her wrist. 'Do you think your wife would like a hand with lunch?' she panted hopefully the next time Mr Burden came within earshot.

He seemed relieved by the possibility of her going.

'I'll come!' I offered before Amelia could, and regretted it instantly, thinking how stupid I was, leaving her the opportunity to impress Robert.

'All right, Biddy?' Mummy went over and leant down, smoothing her hair from her forehead. 'Keep out of the sun, darling. Come on, come and sit nearer the wall. Do you want to come with us, to get lunch? Or stay and wait here?'

Biddy was cross, strands of hair breaking loose from her plaits wet against her forehead. 'I'm firsty.'

'We'll get you a drink, darling, just stay here out of the sun, quietly.' Biddy faced the wall, her lip turned down. 'You've got too hot, haven't you? We'll be back in a minute with something nice to eat and drink. Just wait here with Amelia, be a good girl.'

We went a different way, over a stile in the wall and down the old stepping-stones that had once led children from the schoolhouse at the top straight down to the farmhouse. I let her go ahead of me, rehearsing conversations, smiling, gesticulating, responding to herself.

When we arrived the farmyard seemed deserted apart from the heap in the corner – the black and white sheep dog – which stirred itself and padded towards us disconsolately growling, trailing its heavy head.

'Hel-lo-o,' Mummy called out. 'Mrs Burden – Alison?' and then panicking, turned to me, under her breath, 'That is her name, isn't it?'

'I don't know.'

'Hel-lo-o!' She was heading for the kitchen door and pushed it open gently. 'We've come to ask if we can help?' From behind her I could see Mrs Burden. She had a cigarette in one hand, which she twisted hurriedly into an ashtray. In the other, she held a piece of tin foil that was glinting in the light from the window.

She looked as if she'd been caught out, shaken by the kerfuffle Mummy brought into the kitchen with her.

'How's it going?' she asked, and her face was pulled to a taut smile.

Mummy shook out her arms. 'It's wonderful. Hard work, but it's so satisfying.'

Mrs Burden I thought looked just like a mother should. She began moving sandwiches from the breadboard onto the piece of foil, wrapping them up deliberately like making a bed and transferring them neatly to a basket on the chair beside her.

'Can we help?'

'Don't worry. I'm nearly there . . .'

Her frizzy, wispy hair had no colour. It was pinned up from the back of her neck and then like faded flowers caught in a vase spilled over. She had blue eyes, a bright light blue, and teeth that slanted inwards from where her lips pulled back.

'Actually,' Mummy said, 'do you think I could just use your loo? I've been holding on all morning.'

I couldn't believe how embarrassing that was. I would never, ever ask that – not in someone's house I didn't really know.

'Oh . . . of course you can, it's just up the stairs, there. On the left . . .'

When she left the room, I bit the inside of my lip. Mrs Burden was brushing crumbs from the table into her hand. She was wearing a flowery sort of overall that wrapped in a V over her chest. I didn't expect her to speak to me because she looked so busy. Her voice sounded thin and tight when she asked, 'How's school going?'

'It's all right.'

'Got exams next year?'

I nodded, my jaw moving like wood. I wanted her to like me, more than anything, but I couldn't think of a word to say.

We heard the chain flush, a noise like a plane taking off and the pipes over the sink rattling. We both waited painfully until eventually a door opened upstairs and Mummy, as she came back down, was saying, 'It's such a lovely house! Have you always lived here?'

'Ever since I married.'

'Where before?'

Mrs Burden looked confused. 'Hereabouts . . .'

Mummy was good at seeming interested. 'Are your family from here?'

'The other side of Hexham.'

'Really? Have you a big family?'

'I've brothers – two brothers . . .' She looked unnerved by Mummy's interest.

But Mummy needed no encouragement and I could feel the change of tone in her voice like a drawer opening. 'Mrs Burden,' she said, looking at her as she said her name, 'I wonder if I could ask you something?'

Mummy'd be in a shop, or the library, or the estate agents and tell them the story of her life. She'd tell them how, although she loved the cottage, you could never really live there, not like she'd been expected to do, with young children, certainly not all the time. It was too near the road, there was no water, it was freezing in winter. So often you could see it in their faces: *why's she telling us all this?*

'I was hoping I might catch you. Do say if it's an imposition, if it's too much – or just a nuisance . . .'

Mrs Burden was holding a flask up to her nose. She brought it down and clutched it to her front.

'It just occurred to me. We've – I've got the chance to go with John to Edinburgh for a couple of days and, initially, I'd thought, obviously, I wouldn't be able to go. But then, being here, this time, and Ruth's fifteen, nearly sixteen – very grown-up for her age – I thought if there was just someone to keep an eye out for them, maybe I could . . . They wouldn't need looking after – Ruth can do that fine, can't you? Just keeping an eye on . . .'

The flask dipped a little in Mrs Burden's hands. 'Well, we could keep an eye out for them. Yes, we could. It wouldn't be a trouble. Not at all.'

'Really?' Mummy's eyes were full and excited. 'That would be so wonderful. It really would. Thank you. Are you sure?'

'Yes, certainly, just let me know when.'

Mummy hesitated and looked bashful. 'Say if it's too short notice – you will won't you – and I haven't checked it yet, but possibly even this weekend, if that was OK? Till Monday morning? It's something I feel we really need, now, you know, something like this . . .'

The drawer was hanging open. I wanted to shut my ears. *Not in front of the children!* I didn't want to know, not from her. Knowing in secret was different, picking up the rags and bones of it in the quiet and the dark. I didn't want it from her mouth, direct like that.

'I'm sure it won't be a problem,' Mrs Burden said quite firmly, screwing the lid on the flask.

'Thank you!' Mummy said, wringing her hands in relief. 'Thank you so much – you know you might have just saved my marriage!' And then she laughed when Mrs Burden didn't, as if it really was a joke.

ALISON

12

A lison thought they'd never go, that she'd faint with the mass of them in the room, not the girl so much, but her mother. She sent them out with the basket and the Thermos saying, just to get rid of them, she might follow them later, that she found it hard to function in the heat: it made her dizzy.

She didn't move until she could no longer hear their footsteps; but then she sank into a chair, her forehead in her hands cold as metal. There was something unbearably persistent about that woman, the way she got her foot in the door, her breathiness, the way she flashed her eyes to emphasise what she was saying.

It was a fact that Alison smoked more in the summer when they were around and she lifted her head now to reach for a new packet out of the cutlery drawer. It was a relief to her how a cigarette could still take the edge off things, like sucking a straw, almost a way of proving that she was still breathing; and the smell of tobacco restored the room, banishing that vegetable scent of another woman. She smoked in the same way that she ironed and cleaned and cooked, in a relentless effort to marshal her thinking, keeping the fire lit, keeping things going.

She drew deeply, imagining the smoke putting to rout what lurked inside. At the same time her tongue bent round on itself and dug into the gap where a tooth had recently been pulled, prodding on the bud of an ulcer that wouldn't let her go. Sometimes it hurt too much to eat, or to speak.

August was the worst month. It was the month when the doors and windows hung open, when the days were long and strung out. And it was *his* month: the month he was born, the month he was taken away. Hard enough just getting through, she thought, without the world keep crashing in. If only she could sit still, if only she could tape the entrances and the exits so that the air around her could remain grey and immovable, just until the month passed by.

Her eyes prickled in irritation at the timing of it, the way that whole family descended on the valley, more and more children trampling around, just at the point when it was unbearable again. Two years already since he'd gone and yet, coming back to August, to the sun high in the yard, to the intermittent reek of the pond, it seemed like yesterday.

If anything she felt it more keenly this year than last, winding herself up to a pitch of disbelief at the way that family seemed to muscle in, trying to get involved, the mother in particular. There was definitely something about her that reminded Alison uncomfortably of Eileen, that made her feel there might even be something intentional about the way she pressed herself on her, some aspect of a punishment being served up.

She wondered why the likeness had never occurred to her before. As if, now Daniel had gone, there was nothing to protect her from the world. He had been her surety: her buffer against what people said and what they thought.

When she tried to picture Eileen Bradshaw's features, she couldn't be certain of them any longer – it must be nearly twenty years ago – her face out of focus like a badly taken photograph. She could still see the shape of her though, the way she used to twirl, her nipped-in waist, clapping her hands, because she couldn't believe how little Alison knew (even though she had two older brothers) about boys. It's different, Alison had said, with brothers.

'I should hope so!' And the way Eileen said anything, eyes gleaming, it made you jump with her to a wicked conclusion. *A dirty mind*, is what Graham put it down to.

'You're going to be my project,' Eileen would say, sitting in the bedroom they shared in the nurses' home. 'Let me do you up. You'll look so lovely, please let me!'

She'd never had attention like it, experiencing for the first time the glorious consolation of feeling un-alone. Seeing Eileen in her peach underwear (she hadn't even seen her own mother like that), the blonde pouch of her stomach, her easy way of doing up and undoing a bra. Eileen made it seem from the beginning as if it was just the two of them, and for that brief time Alison felt she'd have followed her to the end of the black night: if Eileen had said jump, she'd have jumped.

When she began to catalogue it, physically, she had to admit there wasn't such a great similarity between Eileen and Lizzie: Eileen a definite blonde; Lizzie more mouse-coloured. But there was something in their manner: the supreme confidence they both had in setting forth (a quality that all through her own life Alison had felt lacking), and they were both attractive and aware of their relative attractions. The very suggestion of a likeness was enough to wrong-foot her, the niggling sensation that perhaps Lizzie might be equipped to detect what Eileen all those years ago had known.

And then – no getting round it – there was Johnny. Right from the start, Eileen's favourite subject had been her elder brother. Stretched out on her bed, she even read to Alison from the occasional letters she had from him, of japes in the quad or at the debating society. You could see she felt his achievements reflected on her and proved that she was made for better things too. When Alison had asked her brothers if they remembered him at school, they'd said he was stuck up. He'd stayed on when they left and then won a scholarship to Oxford, which made the *Hexham Courant*, starting there that same term that Alison and Eileen had begun their training at the hospital.

The Bradshaws had moved from the south – somewhere on the outskirts of St Albans – when their father was ordained as dean at the abbey. According to Eileen, they were always going to return home to where they really belonged, everything in the North being backwards, she'd say, out of touch . . .

It must have been the Christmas of 1961 that Alison finally met Johnny, waiting for him off the train with Eileen in the Railway Bell.

She could hardly believe it, nervous as a rabbit, jumping at every heave of the door because it could have been him. When he arrived, maybe because she already knew so much about him, he seemed fully formed, sure of himself. With his bag pitched over his shoulder he had an energy about him that she'd never experienced, a way of commanding attention and taking on the whole room. At the same time he was easy with them both. He lit up, Eileen pawing his arm, and he turned his cheek to her with the cigarette at the corner of his mouth, so she could peck him there, letting smoke out in a ring. His voice was deep but he seemed to watch them more than he spoke to them, not out of shyness but as if he already knew the power of not speaking. Eileen had pinched Alison's arm in excitement.

It must have been then that he'd suggested taking them both out; he'd borrow their father's car, whisk them off to a dance, 'a bit of social anthropology,' he'd said.

Eileen poised on the front seat with her beautiful hair, sitting like a mother next to a father, Alison crouching like a child in the back. Entering the village hall, he'd kept himself aloof, though he must have known some of the crowd. He only danced with Eileen and then he'd twist slowly down to the floorboards not taking it seriously at all, the two of them laughing together as if no one else mattered.

At the end of a dance Eileen came over, shaking herself from the waist down over her shoes. As she came up, she was fanning herself with both hands. It was the first time Alison had tasted the unravelling sweetness of cider, drinking too much of it, clinging to the cold glass for something to do. Eileen had taken it off her deliberately and then the two of them, Eileen and Johnny, in a conspiracy had grabbed her and one of the farm boys by their elbows and shoved them together onto the floor.

Graham Burden had stumbled into her and had to extricate himself, struggling to get his balance as the music began and there was no escape for either of them. "Til There was You' tinkled in a rhythm impossible to get their feet or their arms around. He fumbled for her hand; they became glued to each other with sweat. And then, like a hot, heavy iron, his other hand through her dress, just below the elastic of her knickers and something in her head bloomed: the hula hoop of her hips as the record circled, the way her dress flared around her, the smell of him, laundered, grassy, his polished round-toed shoes, her pointy kitten heels, clacking, grown-up, and she was aware of the floor slipping like a rug and holding onto him tightly, scrunching the back of his jacket between her fingers. All around the room the others became flattened to the walls as she held on, Eileen and her brother nudging each other, round and round and roundness of holding on in the world, of the sea, of holding on and being watched by Johnny . . .

*

Alison had got into the habit, after lunch, of falling asleep. It was like flipping the switches on the fuse box, shutting down. She found it much easier to trick herself into sleep then than she did at night, when it was often impossible.

For a moment as she opens her eyes, she could be anywhere and there is still the distinct possibility of re-immersing herself in the fuggy, anonymous place from which she has emerged. She blinks, reassembling herself from the ends of her outstretched fingers, wiping the trail of spittle from her open lips, adjusting the top knot on the back of her head where it's been hurting her scalp, pulling sideways. A cigarette butt with its precarious cargo of ash collapses as she draws in her other hand. She starts up and licks a finger, rubbing at the table top, at the brown shadow of a burn that has already marked the Formica.

It can't have been long, but it was long enough to be taken right away, missing the crucial occasion. Except that waking triggers again the whole sickening process of recall and assimilation . . .

She brushes the table furiously with the heel of her hand, hating them for being there, disturbing the peace, squatting along the ridge of the valley as if they owned the place, treading where they shouldn't have been, stirring up the mud. Graham had no time for them. 'Londoners!' he'd mutter and hide in the barn when he heard them coming.

The woman had caught him unawares yesterday and he'd come in raging at them for having nothing better to do. Why should he provide the entertainment? Alison hardly dared tell him what she'd agreed to, being put on the spot like that.

It had become a daily routine, the dog pricking its ears at the children along the river or down from the reservoir, grumbling, then barking, so that there was no real possibility of ignoring them. Often it was all of them at once dragging through the yard, though it was Lizzie who'd begun to go out of her way to have a chat. Even if Alison managed to avoid it, as soon as she was out on the lane, she could feel the windows of the cottage like eyes on her, looking down from above, picking her apart.

That was the other thing: the way Lizzie was, just like Eileen: best friend soon as look at you. And although Alison had learned her lesson in that respect, she couldn't suppress the involuntary reaction to the sound of Lizzie's eager footsteps in the yard, something that in a roundabout way revived the memory of being dropped so suddenly by Eileen, a feeling that was still quite capable of making her smart . . .

In the dark she'd sat with no light on, a towel between her legs. It could have been hours before she heard Eileen's humming up the stairs and her key at the door, the silent question outside as she found it already unlocked, the handle turning.

'Alison? Is that you? What are you doing in here? Turn a light on! I thought you'd be gone – God, you gave me a fright! – What's wrong? You look terrible,' sitting herself next to her on the bed. 'Come on, tell me what's been going on?' There was concern, but there was also a shot of agitation. 'I can't leave you for a minute, can I? Come on, what've you been up to?'

'I'm not well.'

'Have you got a temperature?' Eileen put the back of her hand to her forehead and Alison burst into tears.

'What is it? What's been happening? Tell me!'

'I c-can't!'

'Don't be silly. It's me. You can tell me.'

Alison's mouth looped like a figure of eight, her skin taut with crying. 'It's – It's –Johnny . . .'

'Johnny? What do you mean? What's happened?'

'I can't ...'

'Of course you can, come on. What's he been up to? Have you seen him? Tell me!' Eileen breathed out like a horse in exasperation, 'I can't help if you don't tell me. What's he been playing at?' She'd taken Alison's head and pulled it towards her against the rise of her cashmere sweater, fiddling with her hair, pulling at it as if it were soft tufts of feathers between her fingers.

Yes, she had seen him, although she'd stood back from the window. She'd seen his tallness, standing in a pale shirt, sleeves rolled up to the elbows. She shut her eyes, hardly bearing to think it, knowing perfectly well that it was the one reason this morning she hadn't been able to go out and face them in the yard. *Was she stupid? Had it been staring her in the face all along?* Why had it taken all this time to question the coincidence of names: John, Johnny?

She took a drag from the cigarette and let her head fall, inspecting as a fly would the squirly scratches of the table. Of course she'd seen him before to say hello to, dozens and dozens of times over the years. But, thinking about it – *always with a beard* – such an obvious disguise. She bit her tongue to contain what she was drumming up for herself, but it didn't stop her pursuing the case. John was a university type too; he was bound to be.

She could sit there all afternoon, flicking the lid on the jack-in-the-box, and then packing him away. He and Johnny, even if they weren't the same person, were the same breed, keeping their soft hands for something that would always be considered more important and out of reach of her and her kind.

RUTH

13

I t was Biddy who'd discovered Jack. She'd crept up and opened the door to the bedroom with a whoosh to take him by surprise; and it was better than she could have hoped for, coming across him on his knees, enraged, pummelling his head. 'I *knew* you had nits. I knew it!' and she fled from the room. 'Mummy, Mummy, he *has* got nits, I told you, he's going mad!'

Mummy came to the bottom of the stairs. 'Be quiet!' She lifted her foot onto the first step. 'Jack, darling, are you up there?'

There was no answer. 'Jack?' She began climbing up with Biddy unshakable behind her.

When I followed them into the bedroom, Jack was looking cornered. 'Let me see, darling. Come on,' Mummy soothed. His hands were empty in front of him, his hair sticking up where he hadn't bothered or had time to smooth it down. He was glaring to the point of tears at Biddy who was still hopping around, clapping her hands. There was no escape and he bowed his neck submissively as Mummy knelt down beside him. She took his head between her hands, peering up close, parting the hair between her fingers, turning him towards the window so she could look behind his ears. 'I can't see – no – hang on – keep still, Jack. No. Oh. God, I've found one . . . and another. Oh God, Jack.' Her voice was empty with despair as she sat back on her legs. 'I don't know what to do.'

Last summer she'd taken us swimming in Hexham so that she could use the showers to get our hair washed afterwards. The second time round we got stopped by the attendant, who, in front of everyone spelled it out in a loud, clear voice as if we were deaf. 'They're not for having a wash in. They're not for cleaning hair. You'll use all the water. I'm sorry, but I'll have to say no. I can't be seen to make exceptions.'

Mummy looked paralysed, staring straight down at the floor and we waited for her to say something. Jack had begun scratching as if it didn't matter any more.

I could feel my own head begin to spit with itches. I remembered recently being the only one prepared to sit next to him in the car, feeling sorry for him, believing his denials: I was bound to have got them too.

'I know,' she said suddenly getting a grip. 'All of us. Come on. We're going to wash our hair in the river and then we're going to comb everyone, get rid of them.'

I was so keen to get down there I collected up the towels and the shampoo, calling Biddy and Jack to hurry up. I couldn't believe that we hadn't thought of it before. Part of the misery of the cottage was not being able to wash; of monitoring the increasingly dwindling possibility of being able to be seen by anyone; of secretly visiting the mirror in the kitchen and pressing a finger to make a furrow in an unresponsive head of hair. Grease: the worst evil in the world, when even shopping trips to Hexham couldn't be countenanced.

When we got to the river, Biddy skipping in her frilly-skirt swimming costume, Jack with only his pants, Mummy set up camp on the bank. She took Jack first, pulling him after her into the shallows, holding him by the wrist and dipping the enamel jug into the water at her feet. With no warning, she poured the first load over the top of his head. It was no secret that he hated water, but this time he shrieked as if she were taking out his eyes, turning this way and that in her grasp, flailing out. 'I hate you! I fucking hate you!'

'Jack! Don't talk to me like that!'

'I hate you!'

'Calm down. Come on, if you keep still it'll soon be over, one more.'

She held him ferociously. When he finally wriggled free, rubbing his eyes, staggering over the stones away from her and sobbing convulsively, she called Biddy over.

Biddy was crouched down watching Jack, who seemed stuck in the water, his eyes screwed shut, his hands over his head.

'Biddy, over here! Now!'

She hobbled reluctantly towards Mummy's outstretched hand. 'Good girl.' Biddy bent her head dutifully, standing limply like a soldier accepting his fate. But as the water hit her head and dripped in a waterfall from her long hair back to the river, she shrieked in turn, hunching her shoulders, raising her elbows, gasping for air. Mummy grabbed the shampoo from the pocket of her painting trousers and smeared the green liquid through her hair. Biddy was shaking as if she'd been electrocuted.

'I'll do it. I'm coming, I'll do it myself,' I said hastily, as she looked over at me impatiently. 'Where's Amelia got to?'

Amelia had vanished somewhere between Jack and Biddy's screams. I was keen to get whatever it was over with and keen, so keen to be clean. Jack was still crying and muttering, 'I hate you.'

The jug was almost too heavy to lift and it fell shy of my head. I got a second scoop, half full and poured it face on.

Jesus. It was like being scalped. Like having the top of your head sliced off – like being knocked around the head with dustbin lids. I stood up faltering in the water, river dripping around my neck and shoulders.

I shook the Head and Shoulders bottle upside down and smoothed the paste into my hair. Against the clamp of ice, my kindly fingers and the sharp heavenly smell of the shampoo. I braced myself to rinse my hair, the water like a gunshot, the shock spreading over the whole area of my skin.

Biddy was sniffing and shuddering, trying to grab the towel from Jack.

'Right, let's get back quickly, and we'll use my special conditioner; we'll comb it all out. Come on, Jack.'

'I hate you.'

'I'm only trying to help.'

Mummy was annoyed when Daddy said she looked as if she was enjoying combing for nits. Like a monkey. But she did seem to relish the satisfaction of counting with Biddy the microscopic bodies that were caught between the teeth of the comb, pressing them dead, once, twice, in swathes of bog roll.

All that mattered to me was that I had clean hair, cleaner than it had ever been in my life, metal clean like a brand new head, every shaft 'A-live, a-live o!' I was humming in my excitement, 'Crying cockles and mussels, a-live, a-live o!'

It was as if the whole of me had been dipped in silver. I felt I could go anywhere. In fact, I wanted to be seen. I wanted to shake out the riches of my head in the sun, sparkling, sharp as a pin.

'Wait, Jack,' I said, as he tore away from Mummy still outraged by her, 'I'm coming with you.'

*

I knew exactly how to ingratiate myself with Jack, coaxing him with my interest in his part in life at the farm. He liked to be the one who knew it all.

'So, what happened, with the calves?'

'It was me that brung them out,' he said defensively, as if expecting me to challenge his story.

'I know it was you. Tell me again.'

'Mr Burden let me do it. I was with him.'

'What happened?'

'The first one had its head poking out, and its tongue, and we pulled it all slimy, all black, like out of the river; then Mr Burden noticed there's a second one in there. It'd got stuck, and he put white stuff all up his arm and then he put his hand up the cow's bum and fiddled around for ages and he yanked it and he tied a rope round the hoof bit, and he pulled and pulled, and I pulled behind him holding on like the hugest turnip so when it came out he nearly fell over on top of me – blood everywhere, there was blood all over the place.'

'Blood?'

'A big sack of blood.'

'How disgusting!'

'The cow ate it! I helped Mr Burden when they were lying there. I polished them with straw until they got up.'

'They walked?'

'They walked a bit and then they lied down again.'

'What colour are they?'

'They're not like twins, but they are twins. One of them's black and the other's sort of reddish brown with a white mask on its face and a splash on its back. Mr Burden said because it was me that did it, I could give them names: Batman and Robin, because they're twins.'

'Batman and Robin weren't twins.'

'He said they were brilliant names, and Mrs Burden did.'

I didn't want to annoy him, so I agreed hastily, 'Yes, they are. They're fine names. I'd like to see them. I bet they're *cute*.'

I said the word on purpose, knowing it was illicit, knowing that it would bind the two of us like a shared secret. (What was wrong with it anyway? It wasn't exactly like 'shit' or 'fuck'. Maybe the only reason we couldn't use it was because of what it described: things that were lovable, loved; something I thought, full of grievance at them suddenly, we were meant to do without.)

'They suck your fingers if they like you,' Jack said eagerly.

By the time we got down to the graveyard, my plan was just to be seen by anyone. I'd play it by ear. But I hadn't banked on being ambushed by a whole gaggle of them without a chance to consider my options.

It is so easy to rule people out of your life, and I'd forgotten that Kayleigh and Wendy had ever existed. They used to ride over on their horses, Hero and Biscuit, from somewhere in the next valley. Amelia and Biddy had once made friends with them, playing in the river. I used to spy on their games from behind a wall until they caught me out and Amelia got Wendy to throw stones at me from high up where they were standing on the mill. They gave Biddy chewing gum, which she swallowed and went hysterical because I told her it would glue up her insides. Mummy stopped them playing with us after that. Their father, it turned out, was a maths lecturer at Newcastle. Daddy said he was a pretend farmer and bourgeois. He called them the bourgie kids.

They were bigger than I remembered, with proper haircuts, but still recognisable. Anyway, much worse than that, Robert was sitting with them and they had all seen me: it was too late to turn back.

Kayleigh was older than me, she was probably sixteen now; Wendy somewhere between Amelia and Biddy. They had looked up from the graveyard bench just inside the gate, and they kept looking as we came nearer, Kayleigh with her legs stuck straight out so you could see her shoes, which had a shiny gold metal chain on the bridge of them and Robert who was slouched on the arm of the bench, his long legs arranged in a P, right foot resting over his left knee, chewing a piece of grass. Wendy was spread out picking daisies, rolling to reach them from between the points of her knees.

Jack went and hung by Robert's side as if he belonged to him rather than me. I was on my own, snagged on the gate post.

Kayleigh pulled a smile. 'Hiya,' she said, quite friendly, looking me up and down out of curiosity, smoothing her skirt in a circle around her. It was covered in tiny union jacks like butterflies. Then she turned to Robert as if resuming a conversation, 'Why don't you come? Please.'

'Dunno.'

'It'll be a laugh. Come on.'

I could feel my heart pulsing and I swallowed. My instinct to escape was countered by a new feeling, a contrary rivalry that made me stay. She wasn't even very pretty, I thought. She had a long thin face with a hooky nose and her hair, a wedge at the back, two bushy flicks at the side made her look like Princess Anne. She had on a tight, yellow T-shirt that showed the rumpled lines of a bra. And Wendy, as if they dressed as twins, had the same hair and the same T-shirt, but in pink.

Kayleigh showed no sign of shifting. 'You should get out more, Rob, you're like an old man.'

'And barn dancing's the answer, is it?'

Kayleigh giggled and made her lips into a sort of smooch. She said, 'Beggars can't be choosers . . .'

I listened without saying anything, and the more she sat there, shutting me out, the more determined I became to stay.

She turned to me reluctantly. 'What year are you?'

'O levels.'

'Where's your sister – Amanda?'

'Amelia.'

'Oh, yeah – still playing houses?'

Antagonism made her face uglier and yellow reflected off her T-shirt like a buttercup. She smiled a horrid lick of a smile. 'Have you got a boyfriend?' she asked and I knew she said it to expose me.

'Have you?' I wasn't quick enough and intensely aware of Robert, looking at the ground, chewing, but listening.

Kayleigh smiled again, seeing she'd rattled me. 'Might have . . .' She was looking at her toes again and then coyly at Robert. For a terrible moment I thought I'd stumbled into a trap and a pact; but he wasn't returning her look.

He spat the piece of grass out of his mouth, then lifted his head towards me and my scalp prickled all over, something like the shutter of a camera opening and closing inside. When he looked directly at me I had the feeling that he was at one end of something and I was at the other, like a see-saw.

Kayleigh was examining her baby-pink nails. She began to shuffle in her seat; then she got up casually, smoothing down the folds of her skirt. 'Oh well. Can't sit around here all day. Wend, come on – Maybe see you around?' She glanced across at Robert, and didn't meet my eye when she said, offhandedly, 'Bye, then!'

When they were gone, I wondered if it was worse: I couldn't find a thing to say. How pathetic that I didn't even know how to speak to a boy. It's what came of being at an all girls school, where although we talked endlessly about problems with boys, reading aloud from *Jackie*, putting ourselves into the photofit strips – the mournful face, the turning away, the misunderstanding, the making up, the ecstatic smile; even inventing problems ourselves to send in '*My boyfriend says he'll dump me if I don't go all the way*' – we never actually encountered the real thing.

Suddenly Robert got up, saying, 'Want to come back to ours?'

My mouth was dry. 'OK.'

'Can I come?' Jack asked, in a shrill voice that seemed to anticipate rejection.

'Anyone can,' Robert said, turning with him onto the path towards the stile.

Jack was a good prop, but I was thinking, *He was talking to me, no one in between, just me and him, boy and girl*, and I could feel my head begin to bubble, trying to find the right song for it.

Mrs Burden was at the kitchen table when we went in, with a cigarette like an extra finger. She was playing with the packet.

'How's things, Mother?'

She looked startled, tapping off a length of ash.

'We're going upstairs, all right? Listen to some music.'

She drew herself up and I could feel her eyes on me, taking me in. I smiled at her apologetically, ready to say at the slightest sign of hesitation or disapproval, that I'd go home instead. But she just nodded. 'Not too loud, mind, will you . . .'

ALISON

14

S he lit another cigarette and listened to them bundling into the bedroom above her. It was good to see Robert making friends, behaving like any normal young lad. Alison had nothing against the girl: she was nice enough, polite, quiet. In fact, the children were fine: children were. They hadn't yet learned that in their world her son was unlikely to be considered good enough . . .

How quickly her mind stamped on itself! Two things over which she took herself to task: son came out so easily when it should have been sons. The missing 's' hovering unspoken on the tip of her tongue, irritating it so badly that she wanted to bite it off. How could she have let him go so easily? As if he'd never existed! Daniel: his shy smile, his teeth breaking out of his mouth when he couldn't stop himself, just like his father.

'Sons,' she made herself say out loud. 'My sons . . .' and then squeezed the tip of her tongue against her front teeth until tears stung the backs of her eyes.

And the second thing: the coming up to scratch. It was Eileen's voice she could hear saying: *'Alison, I've no idea what goes on in his head, but don't hold your breath . . . You're a nice girl, but Johnny's got his whole life ahead of him. He's not going to hang around here, is he? He's got his degree to get and then he's free to go wherever he wants. Anywhere! I doubt very much he's going to want to tie himself down, not*

at this stage. How could you think he would? Throw his life away?
Graham's perfect for you, isn't he? I don't see what's wrong. He's a
perfect match!'

There was a grain working away in her head that was defiant.
Who was anyone to say? She listened as the music throbbed above
her, imagining Robert and the face that it was sometimes possible to
trace in him, developing in front of her eyes . . .

Graham had brought her here to live in the farmhouse as soon as
they were married, a room of their own upstairs, but otherwise
everything shared with his parents. It was awkward for her to begin
with, more than awkward. It didn't take her long to discover that her
and Graham's bedroom backed onto his parents' room, only a thin
lathe and plaster partition between. And from the minute she
stepped through the door she was aware of her stomach beginning
to push out, constantly laying her hands against it, fluttering and
drawing attention to it in a way that made his father think she did it
on purpose, to rub his nose in it. When he looked at her sometimes,
she felt like used goods.

'We need a place of our own,' she whispered to Graham when he
came to bed with her.

'It'll be all right. You'll get used to it . . .'

She was bolder when she had him in bed. 'But what if I can't?'

He couldn't help sometimes feeling exasperated by her. 'This is
my home, and I want it to be yours, ours. This is where we live,
where our children will live – I never told you any different.'

When the child came (prematurely it seemed), it took her breath
away. The shock, the violence of it, she didn't think she'd ever get
over. It was like the force of ships being welded together, sheet

metal, heating, smelting, and the seam along her spine feeling that it would be ripped apart like a giant zip. For a week she could hardly walk. She lay in bed on top of a gash that she couldn't imagine ever mending. Her mother-in-law called the midwife because she was worried that Alison wouldn't get up and the midwife advised an immediate hot bath with two packets of salt in it. The smell in the room had become overpowering. Graham didn't like to say. But the midwife agreed, it wasn't healthy.

The baby was kept in a wooden cot next to the bed, mewling, yellow-ish, fisting his mouth, losing weight and still Alison didn't dare look at him properly. The following day the midwife came back with a set of four glass bottles and a box of milk powder. 'We need to beef him up! Mother needs some help!' Alison was relieved to see the bottles empty into the baby like sand through glass, her own milk hard as cannonballs in her breasts, ready to blow her apart if she moved.

They took to him though, despite everything, chucking his chin, and after much deliberation over names, he was called Robert Douglas.

Months after the birth, she slept next to Graham like a board, holding onto the sore between her legs like an easily punctured fruit. Sometimes his hand strayed tentatively onto her, inching up her thigh, pulling her nightdress in little folds so it was like a fan over her buttocks. Graham, his eyes marbling over, leaving her awkward at how to deal with what spilled from him; all the time, his parents listening through the wall, him trying to keep movement to a minimum, to just the squeak picked up by the springs, as if deep in the mattress the reeds of a tiny harmonica had been planted.

She switched off. And when he held her breast and squeezed it roughly until the skin chaffed around her nipple and she wanted to cry out and pressed his hand down firm to stop him, he took it for affection, for pleasure, even.

When Daniel came, twenty-eight months later, she was so eager for him to arrive that she didn't even get to the hospital. He slithered out like a baby seal as she was standing being sick at the sink in the bathroom. She thought then that it would be all right: he was a different child altogether, with his father's nose; he hardly cried.

In her dreams she might be walking high up at Staward Peel, thinking the two boys were with her, but finding herself suddenly alone on the tightrope of a piece of land that shelved steeply on either side of her until it disappeared to nothing, ending before her feet as a great chasm over which she'd have to leap to get to the safety of the tower. It was a hopeless distance to jump, and yet she had no choice, because creeping up behind her, unpicking itself like a thread from a machine, the land was falling away. The distance she measured with her eyes, she realised, was exactly the distance that had elapsed between Robert in his cot and the great body of him now, a head taller than she was, a man's smell about him, a voice that sounded like it had mud in it. The yawning, insurmountable vacuum of a gap was also somehow Daniel; his name echoed in that place in a way that made the birds erupt from all around and caw like a whole army was approaching.

She woke up cold to Robert every time. Ever since he could talk he seemed to have had the better of her. 'Mother,' he teased her, 'don't frown like that!' She ached for him and yet there was something about him that repelled her. He'd recently found himself a Saturday job in Hexham, at the bike shop, and lately he'd been bringing home four-packs of beer, staying up drinking into the night. Graham was against having alcohol in the house and they'd argued about it to begin with, but it was his money and Alison had persuaded Graham to let it rest. Some evenings Graham couldn't resist staying up with him, across from the kitchen table, like he used to with his own father before, and his brother, but this time it wasn't to talk about the farm – the price fetched or not reached – it was an attempt to sit Robert out, to keep him in place.

Last night from her bed it had started with the distant rumble of conversation, mostly the lull between them. But she woke properly at one point in the middle of what sounded like a great tirade. She'd crept out of bed to listen by the door, Robert out of nowhere berating Graham in a fury for being steady, for plodding along, for keeping the whole wretched thing going. 'For what? For those sad knackers in the graveyard? For Dan? For *her*?' She froze at what sounded like an accusation.

'Don't you dare speak of your mother, or your brother, like that in this house. If you're so damn clever, you tell me the alternative – go on! What's the grand alternative?'

'There's never been one. That's the point. You never had a choice, not from the second you were born.'

'It's life – you'll learn that somewhere along the line. We've all got to make a living, one way or another.'

'If it's life, it's a worm's life. You might be happy . . .'

'– and you'll do no better!'

'. . . drowning in shit, eating shit, earning shit.'

'Don't you dare use language like that in this house. It's what keeps you in food, it's what's brought you up. What's wrong with you? It's called making a living . . . an honest day's work.'

'If you say so.'

'I'm not arguing with you. You should show some respect, for once in your life, some gratitude. If you knew the half of what you're talking about . . . You think you can run rings around us, me and your mother, but you're no better than any of us. Drinking that filth! You're not even eighteen – it's not legal, is it? I'm going to report whoever's selling you that stuff, I am, you just give me a name. And when I think! What if your brother was here to have half a go at the life you've got? Has he got a choice? Has he? You've made nothing but a mess of it and everyone around you – look at yourself, drunk! In this house! I'll not have it any longer, do you understand – not under my roof.'

She remembers hearing a noise like the crushing of a can and then Robert, in a low, calm voice saying something that made her bite her fingers: 'It should have been me, shouldn't it? That's what you meant to say. It should've been me.'

When Graham came up to bed, she'd turned away from him, both their hearts churning like engines so that there was no possibility of even pretending to sleep.

'What's wrong?' she said after a while, knowing that she was treading on ice.

'No idea,' he said bitterly, breathing heavily. He was thinking unaccountably about the stray they'd taken in once, a mongrel cross, half sheep dog, half lurcher: Robert's dog. He was going to train it and take it hunting with him. But the dog wouldn't learn. However much it was locked in the shed, beaten, it wouldn't respond. As soon as your back was turned, it would be out, worrying sheep, teasing the cows. Most farmers Graham said wouldn't have thought twice about shooting it. Robert had begged and begged him not to; he'd clung onto his trouser legs and let himself be dragged along the ground. In the end Graham was soft and went out of his way to take it to the dogs' home. But Robert had never forgiven him for it, as if he'd strangled the creature with his bare hands and jumped up and down on his bones.

'Nothing a good thrashing wouldn't have sorted out years ago, if you'd 've ever let me.'

She could feel the twisted crook of his arm as if it were part of a great trunk, felled and careering into the white sheets of the rapids, where she had no option but to follow.

RUTH

15

My heart ties itself into a grand bow, following a boy upstairs, invited, to his bedroom! Jack's ahead of us, bouncing on one of the beds as though he's been here a million times before.

I stay in the doorway as Robert crouches down by the chest of drawers, next to a dozen or so records, flicking through them.

He glances up at me. 'Come in, then. What sort of thing do you like?'

I move forwards but stand awkwardly because there's nowhere but the two beds to sit down; I'm like a stork on one foot and feel myself swaying.

'Anything, really.' I lie.

'There's not much here – can't afford it. My brother got these *Top of the Pops* records for Christmases, 1974, '75, '76 – but they're crap – cover versions anyway. He liked them. I listen more to radio.'

'I've got tapes.'

'Do you like Dire Straits? Status Quo?'

'Not sure . . .' I was floundering. I could picture the men with the sweatbands, the ones with the long hair, and felt a flush of disappointment. There was no getting round it. Perhaps it was just something you had to put up with in boys.

Music is the trickiest subject. There's a divide in our class between disco and mod. Luckily I'm an honorary mod, even though

I've got curly hair: I'm a hippy mod, they say. I've been out on a limb, sticking up for the Beatles all this time against the Bee Gees and 'Ring my Bell', and suddenly, because of the Jam and because Paul Weller wears a badge on saying 'The Who' and because Parkas are in again, I'm the one with the records – the Who, the Kinks – and I'm not fighting any more: I'm all right; and any time I'm asked over to their houses, I arrive with one or two records like a passport smuggled out of Daddy's room.

I sit down on the corner of the unmade bed, next to Jack. Two beds. One of them must have been his brother's. There's the sharp smell of hay, the smell Jack brings back with him to our house, and then something sharper, more chemical that I trace to a black can of deodorant, the white tip of it, the pinprick of its eye, like a lighthouse on the far bedside table.

'I like the sixties,' I say, trying not to sound too hopeful.

'Do you? . . . What about this one then?'

I could see the cover as he brought it out and I almost fainted with relief because I wasn't going to have to compromise after all: the Animals! Robert hunched over, balancing the black disc in his left hand, easing it down over the tall prong of the record player, lifting up the arm and bringing himself close to eye level with the needle, his hand shaking very slightly, coming down with a double 'phit, phit' to the record.

As soon as the song strikes up, recognising the drawl of the guitar, my heart leaps ten times, magnified by the joyful familiarity of it.

'Daniel thought we were related to Eric Burdon – I told him he was our cousin and he believed me.'

'I'd like to be a Burden. I mean' – blushing at what I'd just said – 'related to Eric.' I can't look at him after that and sit as if listening in reverent silence to every word in 'The House of the Rising Sun.'

When the song finishes, Robert hitches up the needle. He seems pleased at my obvious approval of his choice. 'Do you know this one?' He turns the record over, *phut!* The hula hoop of crackly revolutions and then another song springing out of the open mouth of the player. As the song hits my skin the condensation of recognition is like a bathroom mirror. And the voice that speaks is not speaking to me on my own any longer. 'We Gotta Get Out of this Place', raw and urgent, scooping us both up with its promise of flight and new life and I'm brimming over, unravelled, pulled apart and knitted together in a new pattern: a me and a you. I can feel a mercury trickle of sweat tracing its way down my inner arm.

Jack is on his knees on the bed bouncing to a completely different rhythm, face right up to an old poster of Newcastle United, chanting under his breath with each bounce, 'We won the war in 1964, guess what we done, we kicked them up the bum . . .'

But the music that is playing is powerful as an electric fence. Behind it, inside it, tantalisingly within reach, is the dream world I so ache for. I have a picture of it ready, the album sleeve of *Bringing It All Back Home*, Bob Dylan with a cat on his knee, a beautiful gazelle-like woman in a red trouser suit with long dark hair, journals, records, a velvet sofa, looking out, *So?*

I try not to compare it to the unglamorous room in front of me: geometric duvet cover, a pair of jeans shoved under the far bed, a trail of grimy socks, a football boot; on the window ledge, the skull of a sheep with a horn still intact, a biro and a feather in the eye sockets. No bookshelves, just a heap of thick chemistry text books, human biology, a small skewed pile of out-of-date *National Geographic*.

When the record stops, I don't move. Out of the corner of my eye I watch Robert reading the sleeve, balancing it between his thumb and finger, and then I can't help myself. I ask, 'Do you go to school with Kayleigh?'

He looks at me as if I'm stupid.

'Will you go to that dance?'

'Barn dance? You must be joking!'

'Won't she make you?'

'How can she make me?'

'I don't know– if you're *friends*.'

'What, Kayleigh? Do you think I'd hang round with her? Her and her little gang of mates – I wouldn't be seen dead!'

'Where's Daniel gone?' Jack, who had been safely wrapped in his own world, punctures the near perfect resolution of our conversation.

'Jack!' I push him over. 'Shut up.'

He is still bouncing. 'Where is he then? His bed's here.'

'He got run over. By a tractor.' Robert says.

'You know that, Jack,' I say. 'You know that already, don't you?'

There's a silence then that seems to mushroom into every available space.

'Did you get on with him, your brother?' I ask after a bit, forlornly attempting to mend the rift that has opened in the room.

'He was all right.'

'I'd have liked a brother – an older brother, I mean. I can't stand my sister Amelia. They say it's because we were born so close.'

'Daniel always got on better with Dad. He's more like him, wanted to help him out.'

'You help, don't you?' Already, it sounded as if I was defending him.

'Only if I have to. Dumb animals. It's boring. He just can't get his head around the fact that I find it boring.'

'Don't you like animals?'

'*Wild* animals – ones that haven't had the shit kicked out of them, until there's nothing left: meat, two veg, a bag of beef, wool, whatever . . . Wild animals: they're totally different.'

'Jack says you shoot things . . .'

'Only rabbits, crows, rats – It's survival. If I didn't shoot them, they'd be got by something else, by a fox, by mixamatosis.'

'Can you take me shooting? Can I go with you?' Jack bleats.

'If you like.'

'I can't stand the sight of blood,' I say, but add hurriedly, 'I'm not against it – not a vegetarian or anything like that.'

'I'm going to get out of here, soon as I can – I've got to get out, or I'll go mad.'

'What're you going to do?'

He shrugs. 'I thought I'd stay on at school. He didn't want me to, but Mother was all right about it. I'm doing sciences. But I can't really be bothered, not now. I need to get out. I'm supposed to stay on the farm now that my brother's not here; that's what's supposed to happen. But there's no way I'm staying around thinking that it should've been him, they'd all have preferred it to be him . . .'

'Why?'

'He should never have been driving . . .'

'What happened?' I ask it so quietly that he could have chosen to ignore me, but he doesn't. Instead he looks up at me very quickly and then back at the pile of records.

'He was reversing with the trailer on. We were going to move some stuff out of the way and he did it without waiting for me – he wouldn't wait – I could hear the engine from upstairs, and I heard the sound change when it was still going but not moving anywhere.

He drove it back too fast over something – the tractor must've flipped . . .'

'Oh God!'

'He got crushed. He was dead when they cut him out.'

'It must have been so terrible.'

'I should have been driving. It should never have been him . . .'

'What about your dad?'

'He wasn't there. He wouldn't have let him drive on his own.'

'Did he blame you?'

Robert shrugged. 'Anyway, I'm not staying – they can't stop me.'

'Where are you going?'

'Wherever . . . Get a job somewhere, Newcastle maybe. I've got the bike. I can travel. I've a Saturday job in Hexham. They'd take me on if I wanted it, just until I got enough cash saved.'

'I can't wait to leave either . . .'

'It seems weird to me, the people who stay at home.'

'Is he coming back?' Jack pipes up.

'Jack!' I snap, completely infuriated with him. 'He's dead! He died. You know that. He died under the tractor. Why do you think Mum keeps telling you: *don't go near the tractor*. Why does she say that?' I stop suddenly. Robert has fallen slack, sitting back onto his calves.

'I'm really sorry about him – he doesn't understand. Maybe we'd better go.' Robert is staring down and doesn't even flinch when I get up. 'Thanks for the records. I've only got a poxy tape recorder – it eats the tapes! And I miss music when we're here. Thanks.' I can hear myself wittering because it's so difficult to negotiate out of that room, pulling Jack with me, backing through the door, 'Come on, Jack. See you!' onto the landing; 'Bye then.'

*

When we get downstairs, Mrs Burden is still sat at the kitchen table, elbows in front like a tripod. She gives a little jump and coughs. 'All right? Is Robbie there?'

'He's in his room.' (*Robbie*, I think, as if I've dropped through to a new level of acceptance.)

'Isn't he coming down?'

'We've got to get back.'

'Are your mam and dad still going away?'

'Yes, I think so.'

'We'll be seeing you again, then, perhaps at the weekend? Maybe you'd like to come round for your lunch on Sunday?'

'Are you sure?'

'Yes.' She seems to rally pushing herself up from the table. 'Yes, of course I am. That'll be nice. We'll be expecting you . . .'

I chase Jack up the hill, harder than I've chased him in years. 'Moron!' He yelps with glee, thinking he's got me as a friend now and that we are in this together, which, for the time being, I think, doesn't hurt.

I couldn't have dreamed up a better day if I'd tried. Something to tell: I'd been in a boy's bedroom, talked to a boy, listened to records with a boy, smelt a boy. And the stuff at the end, about his brother, and Jack, in a funny way, makes it even better: something shared like he trusted me, something real. James Dean. I'd broken the spell and crossed the line into the world. If nothing else happened, it was enough.

Then I imagine the faces of the girls at school, surprise, interest, gathering round. I'd tell one to begin with, let her think she'd prised it out of me, and then two, letting it spread out naturally. *She's seeing a boy. She did it this summer. Their song. He played their song.*

16

It was half past seven and none of us had wanted to get up. We stood jumbled outside the front door, with jumpers over our nighties. 'You don't mind us going, do you?' Mummy asked, as if it would make any difference if we did.

She was wearing that dress of Mrs Brown's, the thin one, although it had gone brown under the arms. She had a purple and grey striped cardigan over the top of it.

'Come on,' Daddy leant across her empty seat, pushing the door open towards her, 'or we'll never get there. They'll be fine, won't you?'

'We'll be back soon – listen to Ruth, she's in charge.'

I poked Amelia. She scoffed under her breath.

'You won't fight, will you? You'll be OK?'

'Yes, *fine.*'

'Any trouble, go and ask Mrs Burden.'

Daddy was tapping the steering wheel with his fingertips, he turned the key. 'Be good!'

Mummy hesitated again with her hand folded round the door handle. 'We'll phone – five o'clock, all right? Have you got your watch, Ruth?'

The engine was running and revving.

She still had one foot on the ground, thinking, weighing up, then she leant right out and up around the tight angle of the door and kissed us all, straining to reach a cheek or a forehead. 'Goodbye! Be good!'

She might have seen us, until the corner snatched her from view, even Biddy, rubbing where her lips had met our skin.

Once they'd gone, everything was loose – the brakes were off. Amelia and I went back to bed. Biddy began buzzing about, dressing and undressing Arabella. 'I don't know what to do . . .'

I sat up, hung my head and yawned. What joy, I thought, no walks, no collecting wood, no nothing.

'Right.' I roused myself. 'You've all got to do what I say, OK?'

'Piss off!' Amelia woke up.

'You heard her – I'm in charge.'

'La-di-da Gunner Graham!'

We had baked beans and porridge for breakfast. And then I had no firm plan about what we'd do except the vague idea that I might try to put the hands back in the graveyard. I found myself thinking, *What if they died in a car crash? What if Jack or Biddy went missing?* In any case, possessing them had unaccountably taken the edge off wanting them. And I still kicked myself for being so stupid as to let Biddy into the secret: it was only a matter of time before I'd fall out with her and she'd tell.

Amelia was sat on the wall in the garden stripping rushes obsessively to the fragile whites of their insides, which only she had the patience to weave into mats and doilies for the house she'd built against the wall in the field. Jack and Biddy were on the swing. *'Under the Bam Bush, under the sea my darling—'*

'It's Bram. *Bram*. Not *Bam*. Sing it properly if you have to sing it at all.'

'Oohhh, temper, temper,' they chorused. It took a huge effort to ignore them and contain the wave of annoyance as they started right from the beginning *'Under the Bam Bush, under the sea boom boom boom, true love to you my darling, true love to me . . .'*

I bit my tongue. All of them, safely occupied, I disappeared quietly inside, took Daddy's purple duffle bag from the hook on the back of the kitchen door, and crept upstairs out of the front door round to the dump-end of the garden to unearth the hands, shaking off soil and wrapping them up in a teatowel. I came back through the house, stopping off at the bedroom, picking up a jumper for Jack, a cardigan for Biddy, stuffing them in the bag. In the kitchen I made up an empty lemonade bottle with Ribena and took half a packet of biscuits from the bread bin, wedged them down inside and pulled the toggles tight. We might be gone all day.

'Who's coming, then?' I swung the bag over my shoulder, standing in the doorway.

'I'll come.' Biddy had seen me through the kitchen window packing the biscuits.

So it seemed had Jack. 'When are we eating?' he asked

'When we get there.'

Amelia was concentrating on splitting a rush, the tip of her tongue just out of her mouth. 'Where are you going?' she asked, not looking up.

'Wherever.'

'I'll come then.'

I gritted my teeth. 'Fine.'

She slipped off the wall. 'What's in the bag?'

'Nothing, jumpers, food.'

'I'm not carrying anything.'

'No one asked you.'

There was a crackle between us that didn't ever let up. I hated her for making me so unrelenting, so hard-faced. It was exhausting, and, as long as she was around, inescapable. But if I had told her not to come she'd have stuck like glue. My only hope was that she'd get bored. So off we went in a straggly line down the road, Jack, me, Biddy, Amelia.

Past the phone box we turned off onto the track up to the moor. Jack was already scampering ahead, over the first gate. Suddenly on the other side he let out a whoop, throwing back his arms, like he was playing Indians, and a grouse rattled off into the bracken from under his feet. 'Kick it up the arse!' he shouted at the world.

'Bottom, not arse,' I corrected, looking round to see if anyone could have heard.

'You'd know.' Amelia leered, sweeping past me.

'Bitch face.'

'Beast of burden!' That was a new one. I wondered where she'd got it from. Not her usual *Famous Five*.

She was sidling up to Jack, telling him to ignore me, that I was a bossy cow and that he could go and play houses with her if he liked. Then Biddy wanted to go too. Jack began running down the field, chopping the heads off thistles with a stick.

'Where are you going?' I shouted after him.

'Farm!'

'You can't. I'm supposed to be looking after you.'

He ignored me.

'Well, we'll all have to come, then.'

Amelia looked boot-faced. 'There's no way I'm hanging round with you.'

'Do what you like.'

I held on to Biddy and was ready to give her a Chinese burn if she showed any sign of tagging after Amelia. Then I thought better of it and let her go, 'Retards!' I shouted after them, losing my grip.

LIZZIE

17

In the old days John used to drive with his hand on her thigh. She thinks, maybe, if the children are not all sniggering in the back, he will again. They get past Ellersdale and he doesn't make a move. She looks round and puts her fingers up to touch him just below the wrist. He grunts, either 'don't' or to acknowledge it, she can't be sure. She takes her hand away and sighs into her seat. 'It's nice to be on our own, isn't it? It feels like years and years.'

'It is.'

'I hope they'll be OK.'

'They'll be fine. They'll be absolutely fine.'

She's watching the cat's eyes like press-studs, counting the times he seems to cross the line, as if away from her. She's never understood why they don't puncture the tyres. He takes the bends much faster than she does, pulling out of them like a racing driver.

'Bonnie and Clyde'

'Mm?' He turns, fleetingly, to look at her.

She's smiling, looking straight ahead. 'Do you remember, when we drove out of your parents' that time, leaving Ruth and Amelia, so early in the morning it felt like we were Bonnie and Clyde?'

She could still picture the long conservatory steps of the old vicarage, the cacti. 'We were so young, weren't we? You'd never think we'd still be here, four children later.' She held her stomach; it gave way a little, like rubber over water. She'd been so slim, like a rabbit, and now there was a clear pinch of flesh over the top of her skirt, even when she tried to hold it in. 'How did they all come out of me?'

He looked round, for too long this time. She leant forward anxiously and put her hand against the dashboard. She couldn't help herself. Her feet were fumbling for nonexistent pedals, like a driving instructor. He swerved a tiny bit, irritated. 'It's fine – don't do that!'

'Sorry, I can't help it.'

'I'm a perfectly safe driver.'

'I know you are – it's just reflex or something.'

'Can you try not to . . .'

She was biting her lip. 'A child to chiding', that line chose its moments to rear its head and always brought the smart of tears with it. When they were Bonnie and Clyde they could have gone to the ends of the earth, she thought; now she was holding on by her nails, clinging on, determined not to look down. *Don't look down!*

Furtively she catches herself in the passenger mirror, lifting her chin a little. Her face, paler than it should be at this stage in the summer, but, she thinks approvingly, not uninteresting. She lengthens her neck and makes an effort to straighten her shoulders, sitting poised in the seat, letting herself rehearse the possibilities that the mirror opens before her.

When she is left to sort out the mess of his comings and goings, without any answers, without any way of explaining with any dignity at all why he has gone, she can recount to herself a story that shows she too has a choice, that there's a life outside John and that if he doesn't begin to notice, someone else just might – they just might. And then he'd be sorry.

The time after he'd stormed off, earlier in the summer, she'd been out in the garden, in the deckchair, her skirt around her thighs, legs wide apart, trying to get them brown. She was determined to finish *The Woodlanders*, although the sun on the page was too bright and she was being tormented by her last argument with him, rewinding it endlessly in her head, gazing straight out into the hedge, or shutting her eyes on it, wondering whether maybe she had over-reacted, whether he was right and she had a destructive streak that just wouldn't let things be.

When she heard the gate click, it made her jump. She felt silly, thinking, it could only be John: they didn't ever get visitors. But it wasn't. It was someone quite different, dressed in denim, with his hand on the gate. She pulled down her skirt hurriedly.

'Hello, there!' He raised his hand.

The denim matched his eyes. For a minute she thought, he could have been Jesus: shoulder-length hair, beard. Amelia, who'd been arranging her china all along the wall looked up at him with her mouth open. Lizzie pushed her hair back, and put her book face down on her lap, her face burning. 'Hello.'

'I'm Marcus, do you remember, we met . . . ?'

'Oh yes . . .' She bent forward, desperately trying to place him, struggling in the deckchair and almost upturning it as she got out. 'Yes, of course I do, the Laing, private view – yes. Hello.'

He'd walked all the way from Bridge End, where he was renting a cottage, he said.

'That's miles, isn't it? Would you like a cup of tea or something?'

He set his knapsack on the bench and pulled out a bottle of wine. 'Is it too early for you?'

'God, no, that would be nice!' Lizzie's smile was so broad it showed the gaps between her teeth right at the back. 'Come in! I'll just have to try and find a corkscrew.'

He followed her into the cool air of the kitchen and she began rummaging in the huge drawers of the dresser.

'I've got a penknife here, if you can't find it.'

She turned round and sighed in relief. 'I don't know where it's got to – We hardly use it.'

He brought out the cork with an extravagant lift of his arm and poured the wine into tumblers. 'Cheers!'

'Happy summer!' she said.

Then he got out a packet of Gauloises and offered her one. Although she didn't smoke, she took it, looking straight at him, her hand trembling like a teenager's. When he held out a match, she stuffed the cigarette between her pursed lips. It didn't light. 'Could you do it?' she said and he took it from her, holding it in his lips for a while, slowly raising the match, cupping his hand around it. 'Here.' He handed it back to her.

'Thanks.' She took it and put it straight to her mouth, sucked hard, blowing out smoke like she was blowing a dandelion clock. Then she was talking fast and garrulously as she always did with other people. She finished, 'I'm not used to talking any more – just to the children – we've not seen anyone else for days. Sorry – I'm burbling.'

Marcus cocked his head as if he was taking her in, then he shook it, laughing, his hand wafting away a trail of smoke. 'Not at all.'

'What brings you out here?'

He told her how he spent half the time at Bridge End, painting, and the other half teaching art at the poly in Newcastle.

They came outside and she moved a paper to make a place for him next to her.

'What's John up to these days?'

'This and that, still writing for the paper – he's been to London to see some exhibition, but he'll be back soon.'

'It's a great place you've got,' he said, looking around.

'Yes, I love it here,' and, saying it, she felt she could love it.

'Do you come here often?'

She could feel herself reddening at the implication he was chatting her up, curiously inflated, as if she could skim water. 'In the holidays mostly, since we moved to London, it's too far to come for weekends now.'

'You don't regret moving?'

'No, I don't think so. Not really.' Then she said, hardly able to suppress the smile, 'I've started to write.'

'Have you? That's fantastic! What sort of thing?'

'Nothing really, bits and pieces. But I've been going to a class and it's been just wonderful. I love it!'

'So when are we going to see your name in print?'

'Oh, never, probably. But doing it, I just love having something to do outside of my life.'

When the car drew up no one heard it. Amelia had brought out her knitting and was offering it to Marcus. He said no one had ever knitted for him before and he was deeply honoured. Amelia was beaming. She wrote in her diary afterwards that she'd definitely marry a man with a beard. Now she lost some of the stitches, she was so keen to get it off the needles and into Marcus's hands. He felt in his pocket, leaning to one side to reach right in. 'Here,' he said, drawing out a coin, 'have this.' It was a brand new fifty-pence piece.

'It's not fair!' Biddy was looking at Lizzie, pleading.

'It's Amelia's scarf. If Marcus wants it, that's up to him.'

'I'll make you something,' Biddy said, edging herself off the bench. As Lizzie's eyes followed her to the kitchen door, thinking of a way to distract her, she heard the familiar thunder of John's boots on the stairs and an instant later he burst out into the garden looking startled at the additional body.

Lizzie had already raised a glass in his direction as if to shush him. 'It's Marcus,' she said, nodding over at him emphatically. John looked uncovered; he said stiffly, 'Good to see you.'

She asked if he'd like some wine.

'No. No, thanks – not after the drive I've had. In fact, I've got a bit of a headache. Do you mind?'

'Don't be anti-social John.'

'I think you mean unsociable.'

'I know what I mean!'

John was pallid compared to Marcus, but otherwise not dissimilar. He was tall and gangly with a beard, but he had glasses too, which in Lizzie's eyes made him look intellectual, like John Lennon. The children didn't like it when he took his glasses off. It made him look like a baby, bleary eyed and lost.

Before Marcus went, Biddy came back with something behind her back. She produced, like a fanfare, a hastily composed drawing of a girl and a flower. 'For me?' Marcus said he loved it although he didn't have anything left in his pocket.

'Oh, don't be silly, she doesn't want anything for it.'

'Next time, I promise, I'll come better prepared.'

It was awkward then, Lizzie urging him to stay and have supper and Marcus waiting to be pressed by John. John studiously ignoring what was going on, taking an uncharacteristic interest in Jack and his day. Marcus smiled a little regretfully but said extra-decisively, 'No, I'd better get going. It's a fair way home and I want to get back before it gets too dark. Thanks, though, for asking.'

He said goodbye to John and Jack downstairs, but the others followed him in a muddle to the road and when he set off, they stood and watched until he came to the corner and turned around, waving like a sailor, one more time. Lizzie turned to go in; she was seething when she reached the bottom of the stairs.

'You could have made a bit more effort.'

'How was I to know he'd be here?'

'He turned up. It didn't stop me being nice to him.'

'It didn't look as if you needed any help.'

'What do you mean?'

'Forget it.'

'And don't criticise me in front of people like that . . .'

'What did I say?'

'You know perfectly well – It doesn't matter. Just don't do it. Don't do it again. Anyway, where have you been?'

'You know where I've been.'

'I don't. I've got no idea.'

'Not now. I'm back. Not now.'

Why shouldn't she ask him? She had a right to know. But the wine, which had seemed such a release, now made her head feel clamped and tired; her tongue like leather in her mouth. 'Can you just keep away from me, then, please?'

She went upstairs on her own. It gave her time to reflect, to weigh up his expression; perhaps his crossness could be translated as jealousy? What a wonderful thought! To extract just a pinch of the jealousy she'd been tormented with over the last year. And if he could still be jealous, there must be life in it. There must be something to save.

It was nearly eleven when they reached Edinburgh and half an hour later before they found Melville Terrace, a crescent with a B & B that the secretary from the paper had recommended. It was Festival time and a shock to the system – all those people crowding along Princes Street. She had even felt exposed in the car, jostled, but Melville Terrace was quiet and leafy, with large vacant brown windows.

'I'll show you to your room,' the woman said briskly, after writing their names in her book. She smelt of apricots. She had on a beige twin-set and a tweed, herringbone skirt, very pink lipstick.

'It's awful busy, isn't it? Have you had a long journey?' She seemed to chop her way up the stairs.

'Yes.' John was always monosyllabic and Lizzie over-compensating, smiling at her profusely. 'We've come down – up – I never know which – from Northumberland.'

'That's a nice part of the world.'

'We love it there. But we live in London.'

The woman was concentrating on her clutch of keys. 'Here we are.' She held open the door and bowed them past her into the room. 'I hope you'll have a comfortable stay.'

Twin beds. Straight away Lizzie's heart sank. Counterpanes, floral valances. It reminded her for a second of her parents' house. She wondered if John had booked it on purpose.

She slumped down on the corner of one of them. 'Twin beds!'

John let the bag drop. 'Never mind, we can put them together if you want.'

'I don't mind,' she lied, feeling tearful.

'Come on, it's not a disaster. It's easy!'

She showed no sign of moving. It even smelt of her mother's room, of those twin purple candlewick counterpanes, of her cream and lace nightie always neatly wrapped at the end of her bed like a cat.

She sighed more heavily than she meant to and got up to hide her eyes by staring out of the window. The building overlooked a communal garden, fenced in with railings, green with trees, the odd car nosing around, one way and then back looking for a place to park.

She couldn't understand why despite being so high up she felt submerged, like being in a diving bell. Disappointment. There was a time they'd have bounced on the beds like children, explored every nook, every drawer, laughed together at the paper doilies on the tray, the tassels on the curtains. Now urgency and curiosity seemed to have deserted them.

'Was this such a good idea?' She said it, she thought, in an even voice, but couldn't help sounding recriminatory.

'Don't start! Come on, I've got to find the office, get tickets, catalogues. Are you coming?'

She could quite happily have stayed there, arrested, shackled to the window ledge, letting the brown air wash through her. But she roused herself in a supreme effort. 'OK, then, let me just have a pee.'

18

They'd done the National, the Royal Academy, the Fruit Market, the Portrait Gallery, and walked all the way to the Botanical Gardens and around the Museum of Modern Art when John said he needed to go back to check names, dates, the juxtapositions: he had to get it right. Lizzie's legs ached, and she agreed to stay and wait for him in the gardens. Watching him disappear like a stranger she instantly regretted letting him go.

It was a beautiful day to be outside, late afternoon light, stolid family groups: children playing, fathers folding pushchairs, mothers packing and unpacking crisps and bananas. She sat down near a rhododendron bush and brought out her red notebook so that it looked as if she was doing something. She tried not to think that, for all the difference it would have made, it might have been better if the children had come after all.

She forced herself instead to pull something of use out of the paintings and sculptures they'd paraded past that day. There was only one that had really struck her, right at the end. John had caught up with her as she stood in front of it and she'd pointed out to him, right in the corner, a fly that had been swept up in the paint. 'Don't touch it!' he'd said fiercely, as if to a child.

'I wasn't going to touch!'

Anyway, he shrugged semi-apologetically, yes, of course he had noticed it: a small fly hijacked by a lick of paint. By now she was feeling petulant and kept on, determined not to be put off, asking him like an over-eager student if he thought it was meant to be there, if he thought that Pollock might have looked, in retrospect, and laughed at the way the fly had gatecrashed his painting and had maybe brought to it an unsought-for significance? 'Like Icarus,' she persisted excitedly, 'you know that Auden poem, I can't pronounce – 'Musée des Beaux Arts – I can't pronounce it! "The ploughman may have heard the splash, the forsaken cry . . ."'

John was looking around, wincing; he turned away from her and mumbled something she couldn't hear.

It incensed her when she tried to get him talking about things that mattered to her – things that by definition had nothing to do with what had preoccupied the last fifteen years of her life: children, cooking, cleaning, decorating – all the things she knew very well he had an interest in, but for some reason excluded her from. He, of all people, who should support her, who prided himself on the thrust of his critical faculties, greeted her attempts with cold water, refusing to take her seriously.

To him, there was something repellent about the urgency of her newfound thirst for knowledge. He said again that it embarrassed him talking in front of paintings.

Her doodling was beginning to break through the paper. She turned the page, two pages, to a clean sheet and began to write: *Number 49. Icarus. A fly in paint. Tangled in paint. The boy from the farm. A man hanging. All of us – flies and all.* Her writing was jagged, uncharacteristically large, and she looked at it through the thick lens of tears that sat on her eyeball. *Meaningless.* She tore it out. *I can't write!*

And yet it was like graffiti, a basic urge, so that moving the pen, even to scribble, even in hopelessness, was a tiny and comforting proof to herself of her presence in the world. It was as if her life depended on it. And so, for want of what to say, of failing, she began mechanically to write out the last and the favourite of all the poems she'd learnt by heart, 'One Art', aware, grimly, that it would be an act of masochism as well as comfort. She knew it, like peeling an onion, taking off the top layers, cutting through to that last verse, making herself write neatly and evenly,

> — Even losing you (the joking voice, a gesture
> I love) I shan't have lied. It's evident
> the art of losing's not too hard to master
> though it may look like (*Write* it!) like disaster.

How satisfying in a strange sort of way, she thought, to be able to summon tears on demand.

It was so hard to get things straight in her head: impossible to know whether to believe anything John said, or to hope that she wilfully maligned him and that she was creating something where there was nothing. She missed being able to talk to her friend Caroline, who lived along the road from them in London, and her unequivocal pronouncements on the conduct of men. John had never got on with Caroline, with what he regarded as her interference and the raising of his wife's pretensions. She had befriended Lizzie when they first moved and helped her get her bearings. She had introduced her to the notion of treating herself, showing her the stall to look out for in the flea market in Brixton, under the railway bridge, the tall, oddly distinguished-looking man in a beige overall who set out his table long after all the others, unpacking huge parcels of clothes done up in canvas. There was always a throng of women agog at what he might unfurl but he wouldn't be hurried, slowly releasing a cord and shaking out among the small fry, gold lamé, cashmere, Yves Saint Laurent. And the second-hand treats Lizzie would bring back, buried at the bottom of heaving shopping bags, loaded with a week's worth of bread, potatoes, fruit, mince, that she wouldn't show him until she'd tried them on in secret, and then in front of Ruth or Amelia, keeping the rejects in a bag hidden under the stairs. For a time it was the highlight of her week.

Last year, it was Caroline who'd persuaded her to go with her to an English literature class at Morley College. In the spring, emboldened, they'd switched to creative writing. Lizzie had been surprised at how easily she could fill pages with her neat and dense script. Soon she had half a dozen notebooks under the bed, held together with elastic bands, with bits of envelopes or tickets sticking out where she'd been caught by an idea on the bus, or in the middle of the market.

The desire to put things down, anything, had been like a rediscovery, something reclaimed from the first glorious moments of true privacy in her own bedroom as a thirteen-year-old, a five-year diary which she kept religiously for two months when she was going to be everything: an opera singer, an artist, a writer, the wife of Ernest Hemingway. Then the wilderness years of having children, of having to remember spelling tests, prize-givings, piano exams, nit-combing, nativity plays.

It was like shooting up from the ocean bed to breathe luminous air, of extricating herself from the four black holes that followed each blurred and dreadful birth, the years of trying to get the house straight on no money, the painting, the endless mixes of Polyfilla squeezed into the cracks . . . It had been feast after famine and she'd resolved to live in the future on a bare minimum of domestic drudgery and cram as much as she could read and write into every remaining corner of the day.

The last three weeks of the class had been taken by the poet, Martin Cruickshank, who'd got them to study and memorise a single poem each time: Auden, Larkin and Elizabeth Bishop. This had been an even greater revelation. Before that, poetry had meant nothing to her – it was either abstruse and beyond her, or da-di-da with facile rhyme. She revelled now in how misguided she had been and took delight in measuring just how far she'd come: how amazingly satisfying it was to puzzle over and unpick meaning, like cracking a code; and, having broken in, how a poem could admit her to the big swim of things, where everything stood for something else, where it was possible to consort with gods and trees.

Now it was the best part of her week to hear Philip Larkin reading 'Whitsun Weddings' on the radio, and she carried around with her the first poetry book she'd bought, Ted Hughes' *Crow*. At the last class, to forestall the goodbyes, Martin had invited them all to a reading he was giving at the Poetry Society the following week, and she felt herself shake with excitement at the possibility of an entrée to a world that until recently she had never dreamed of coming within orbit.

It was a blow when Caroline was ill and couldn't come with her. But she surprised herself at how determined she was and made herself take the three buses necessary to get from Brixton to Earls Court, on her own, terrified.

She found the building at the corner of a grand-looking square, like a private house with a brass plate on the door. A small huddle formed behind her on the steps and it quickly became too late to retreat. She entered the hallway and attached herself to the trickle of people trailing downstairs to a dreary, narrow room with a bar along one wall. At first she couldn't recognise anyone from the class and felt sickeningly out of her depth; her lip began to tremble as she sought frantically to find a reason to leave, until, from over on a high stool at the bar, she was aware of someone, Martin himself, beckoning her over, and then insisting on buying her a drink. 'Cheers,' he said, smiling encouragingly, touching her elbow, and he turned to the bearded man next to him. 'Meet my Irish friend – poet, philosopher – Matthew Sweeney. Matthew, let me introduce a budding writer from south of the river.' She was confused by the hyperbole of his introduction, but couldn't help herself – though she shook her head – glowing, raving from the inside at the 'budding writer', white wine swilling to the extremities of her glass.

After the reading, one of the other three poets on the platform, a Russian on his way to America, came to where she was still standing nervously at Martin's elbow. He was a different species of man, tall and stooped in dark layers of thick clothing. When he spoke, looking at her, but congratulating Martin on a poem of his about making soup after his mother died, it was in the same exotic way he'd read his own work, a purring, musical voice, like Dr Zhivago.

It took one disastrous lack of concentration for the glass in her hand to fall straight through her fingers and shatter onto the parquet floor. Before she could draw breath, the Russian, catching her eye, had calmly held his own glass out in front of him and opened his hand, letting his glass hit the same spot on the floor, so that the fuss of running for a cloth, a dustpan and brush, of picking up the tiny pieces, was entirely diverted from her. He said nothing, but smiled, and her mouth fell ajar in gratitude, thinking, if he had only asked she'd have disappeared with him then and there.

It was late when she had left for home, silver with rain, but dark. They hailed her a cab, though she protested, elated, that it was fine to get the bus. When she got back she had to go into the house frantically searching for money, leaving the taxi making a racket out in the street. John was already in bed. She was sick downstairs; she hadn't eaten all night.

The next day he mocked her and told the children she'd been drunk. She didn't bother disputing it because their teasing was a way of keeping the picture of herself as a mover among poets alive and real. The day after that, she wrote a poem herself about a strange conversation in two unrelated languages that ended with the image of a shattered glass. She brought it to John, shyly, like one of the children. As he took it from her she recognised the got-at frown on his forehead, and a minute later he handed it back, nodding. 'Yes.'

'What do you think?'

'Fine – yes, good.'

'But you haven't read it – not properly.'

'Yes I have.'

'What does fine mean?'

'What do you want me to say? I'm afraid I haven't got the lingo of your fellow classmates.'

'Is there anything in it you don't like?'

He took it from her again and cast his eye down the page, 'No, um . . . no. I don't think so . . . the "she" is you, presumably?'

'Well, yes. But it's not supposed to be just about me.'

'It's fine. I don't know what else I can say.'

'Whether you like it or not.'

'I've said so.'

'You could sound as if you meant it.'

'For God's sake – I don't ask you to look at my pieces.'

'You used to. I've typed enough of them up for you.'

He had taken a deep breath and she could see the muscle in his cheek twitch. His glasses were like a dark skin of water, reflecting her back to herself. He was beyond reach, obdurate, taciturn as if her voice, her hand, could pass right through him.

She must have closed her eyes for a minute on the violent ends of the red sun. The edges of things furred with light: trees, bushes, burning. She clung to the notebook as if it were her only means of maintaining her existence in the lengthening shadows, filled suddenly with the annihilating sense of having been misplaced or left behind.

RUTH

19

I watched Amelia and Biddy over the gate, back down the track, past the phone box, around the bend in the road. The duffle bag was cutting into my shoulder. I sat down, pulled it open and brought out the bottle of juice. I took a swig and then poured the rest, hicupping out of the neck onto the track, watching it creep away in rivulets between stones, into cracks, chasing beetles out over the dry earth. The empty bottle collapsed and crackled in my hands as I stuffed it back and restrung the bag over my head. I knew it was only a matter of time or prompting before Biddy would deliver my crime to Amelia and I decided to follow Jack down towards the farm, hoping I'd find some chance to slip the hands back, ready to deny the whole episode.

The grass and the buttercups were growing above my knees, harbouring flights of crane flies that rose towards my face and I found myself wading, concentrating only on lifting my arms and feet as if I were for a moment one of the same species, the warm breeze urging us all downhill. When the sound of the river began to interfere, it brought a current with it and I felt a rush of excitement. In the same moment I caught sight of Jack and Robert over on the opposite bank. My heart bounded. Robert was skimming stones across the water, Jack counting the skips for him and congratulating him with a running commentary.

They both looked up at me, Jack crossly, Robert's wide face falling open into a smile. 'Are you coming over?'

I made my way to the edge of the bank.

'It's not deep, not over there.'

I had plimsolls on and he must have seen me considering my feet, and looking across at the water and hesitating. He must have seen me wanting to come, like wanting to jump into the swimming pool but needing encouragement and someone to watch me.

I stood teetering, measuring down and across and across and down as if getting there would be as impossible as being able to jump it in one giant leap.

'Hang on a second. I'll give you a hand, if you like.' Before I could say anything, he bent down and rolled up his jeans. Jack's face clouded in disapproval. I was paralysed by the idea, but seeing as I didn't stop him, Robert began wading over. 'You'll get wet!' I shouted famously.

He was arriving and I couldn't begin to think of a reason for him not to, his body buffing up towards mine, pushing the air out of the way between us. He hardly stopped for breath, bending over with his elbows braced out, his hands set firmly on his thighs. 'Ha'way, then!'

I looked at the stretch of his back. 'Are you sure?'

'Course. Hop on.'

My hands hovered above his shoulders without touching them. He peered around. 'Go on, then.'

'I don't think I can jump.'

He bent lower. 'Come on, it's easy. Yes you can.'

I hesitated again, like sizing up the horse in the school hall, and then I put my forearms around the base of his neck.

'Ready?'

I played for time, pretending to count to three, bobbing on my knees. He lurched forwards as I jumped and at the same time hooked his arms under the backs of my legs and shunted me with a grunt further up his back.

'I'm too heavy, aren't I?' my voice was shrill with embarrassment.

'You're all right. Just hold on.'

He staggered forwards into the water trying to find a foothold. I squeezed my eyes and stretched my mouth, holding onto my breath as if it would make me lighter, releasing it in fits of nervous laughter. His foot slipped and we wobbled. He stood stationary for a minute to get his balance and then we made our way into the stream, step by step, slipping, countering, me trying not drag him down, to shake, Jack on the opposite side longing for us to topple over.

Once I'd adjusted to the shock of it, of being lifted off the surface of the earth, of clutching onto his T-shirt so that it pulled up, the warmth of his bare skin seeping right through to me, I began to want it never to end. I was overwhelmed by the smell of him, cancelling out all worries of my own smell. Like under a microscope I watched the pores of his skin along the back of his neck, the black silky fringe of hair, the burnished skin as it met his T-shirt and I wanted to lick or bite to make a mark. My legs were like tongs gripping around him, with a burning coal at the join where they opened and shut. It felt as if he had lifted an impossible weight from my shoulders, a cloud of waiting for something to happen, of fighting, of bossiness; and the lightness took everything away to just the seed of me, the X marks the spot of me.

I clung on when we got to the dry pebbles on the other shore and he stood as upright as he could to get me off. 'Thank you.' I was dizzy, trying to readjust to gravity and ground, holding onto the cord of the duffle bag as if it was a parachute that would save me from falling. 'I must weigh a ton.'

'You're all right.'

'Skim another stone,' Jack demanded. 'Come on, let's do another one.'

His arm was strong and like elastic as we watched him whizz a flat pebble, one, two, three, four, five times, stitching the water.

'Jack,' he said after a bit, shuffling a pebble from one hand to the other, 'why don't you go and make a den?'

Jack looked affronted as if he was being turned in to the police. And then sullen.

'We can go out later, if you like?'

I could see Jack weighing his options and reluctantly, bitterly, caving in. He glared at me, his jaw rigid, and then he retreated, scuffing his boots all the way, the square thumb of his head set to the path, hopping as he got nearer the stile towards the farmyard.

We watched him until he disappeared from view and there was no reason to keep looking; so we turned to each other and it seemed as if we were two people stepping out in the snow for the first time.

'I'll show you something,' Robert said, leading me in the direction of the graveyard. I was so close I had to put my hands out in front to balance, almost touching his back to stop myself falling. We wove a path between the old graves, to the back end of the chapel. He was heading towards the group of tombstones that leant around in the shadow of the far wall. 'It's Burdens, all over here,' he said, 'practically as far as you can see.' Then he dropped down and began tracing words with his finger on a thick stone that was blistered with lichen, reading out, 'Robert Alfred Burden – that's my father's granddad. I was named after him, supposedly.'

'What did he do?'

'Farming – like all of them, his dad, and his dad's dad . . .'

'Not you, though?'

'Who knows . . . maybe I'll have to.'

'Why?'

'Someone's got to.'

I didn't know what to say. I was scrabbling around and before I thought, it came out, 'Is Daniel – your brother – is he buried here?'

Why had I said that? Robert looked up before I could take it back. Then he said, 'There's not a stone or anything yet. He's over there somewhere, in the short grass with the newer ones.'

It felt as though I was walking on a string bridge that might collapse at either end if I put a foot wrong.

'You could still go to college.'

'Maybe . . .'

'You might find out what you really want to do.'

Robert shrugged. 'What're you doing?'

'I don't know. A Levels. Leave home. College maybe . . .'

'Don't you like London?'

'Not London; my family.'

I felt a rush of wanting to confide in him, of separating myself from them, and of having my own story to share with him. 'I think they're going to split up.'

'Why?'

'My mum thinks Dad's got someone else . . .' As soon as I said it, I felt the sordidness of it, and the possibility that in some way I was tarring myself with the same brush.

'Has he?'

'Don't know.'

'But he wouldn't leave, would he?'

'People get divorced . . .'

'Not if they've got children.'

'They do.'

'I don't understand that.'

It seemed then as if my heart would burst. We were sitting cross-legged like infants in assembly, our knees just touching. His eyes were such a dark brown, they looked black. I could see the raw skin on his cheeks, the smattering of hair on the nub of his chin like pepper. It had gone so quiet that I was breathing through my mouth, very shallowly. The sun was coming in streaks between the clouds through the spokes of a giant bicycle wheel that turned and turned. The closeness was like nothing on earth, blotting out everything to just the grind of river, the hissing of grass, the trees all swirling.

Suddenly, like a twig rattling the spokes of a wheel, a voice cried out, 'Robbie! Robbie!', urgent and quick and there was a desperation about it that made us both start up.

20

'Rooooo-berrrrt!' This time it was long drawn and desperate, a name, like God, to shout out.

'What do you think it is?' Robert asked me.

'Maybe we'd better go.'

I was relieved in one way, and got to my feet, brushing grass seeds from my skirt and pushing hair behind my ears, grabbing the bag and then following him, keeping to the imprint of his boots to avoid the nettles, raising my elbows above them. When we got over the stile, Robert yelled out towards the farmyard, 'What is it? I'm here!'

We could see Jack at the far end, near the old mill. He turned on his heel. 'Robbie!' he said with relief, and came stumbling towards us.

'I didn't do it, Robbie, it just happened. I didn't do it – I didn't do anything.'

'What? What's happened?'

'It wasn't my fault. I didn't do it.'

'Tell me what's happened.' Robert's voice was like a wall and Jack stopped against it.

'Jack,' I said, 'just tell us.'

He looked at me suspiciously and then at the ground.

'We won't be cross.' I caught myself sounding just like Mummy.

He looked up like he had something stolen hidden behind his back and knew he'd have to hand it over. He hesitated, then muttered, 'Batman.'

'What about Batman?' Robert was walking backwards towards the stable as he said it and Jack started again, 'It wasn't my fault, I couldn't stop him, he must've got out, and he just went on and on.'

I pulled him along beside me as we followed Robert round to the dark entrance of the barn. 'Where is he, then?' Robert said.

I peered in. Robert was pushing a metal barrier back to shut off the pen. There was one calf in there backed up against the wall.

'I just opened the gate a tiny bit, to get some water . . .'

'Where is he?'

Jack was rubbing his nose with his fist. 'I didn't do anything. It's not my fault.'

'Just tell me where he is!' Robert shouted, and I was vicious, furious that Jack had ruined everything. 'Jack, tell him!'

I could see tears mounting in his chest as he lifted his arm stiffly and pointed towards the mill.

Robert followed the line of his finger. 'Where?'

The three of us began to make our way towards the great granite wheel and the rusty cogs of the old mill machinery. The pond water was brackish, the colour of dark tan tights.

'Are you saying he went into the pond?' Robert asked neutrally, as if the answer could easily be no.

'I couldn't stop him, I couldn't. I was scared of him. I saw him sinking down and making a noise and bubbling. His eyes were all funny. I couldn't get him out, I told him to get out but he wouldn't, he was slipping all over and he wouldn't get out . . .'

Robert began to unlace his boots. He kicked them off.

'Get a rope,' he said, lifting his shirt over his head, 'from the shed.

Now!' Jack ran and disappeared. He came out with a coil of dirty orange cord in his hands. Robert ran to meet him and grabbed an end. He tied it to a metal post, measured out a body length and then looped the rope around his waist, like a knitting needle, casting on. Then he plunged out into the water.

The surface smashed and bubbles began to rise all around him. He gasped. He was up to his thighs already and began casting around with his arms, like pretending to swim, then up to his waist.

'Be careful!'

He ignored me, concentrating. Then he said something under his breath.

'What is it?'

His head was perfectly still, his eyes staring straight out, but under the water his arms appeared to be latching on to something. 'I . . . got it . . .' he was talking to himself, manoeuvring under the water. 'I've got him . . .' bending down as far as his chin and still staring straight ahead. He seemed to be folding his arms around, rolling the water. When he turned, the pond threw a wake around him. He took two or three lurches towards us, and hauled himself out. He was plastered in mud, stinking, but he didn't stop. Reaching for the rope, he began to haul, hand over hand.

At first the rope gave easily, then the tension of it flicked brown water into his face. He leaned right back with his feet against the post, as if he were on a ship, using his weight to pull and tug, wrestling the rope, inch by inch, from the water. Suddenly, something seemed to give, and turning my head away, into Jack, I had the impression of some grotesque masthead rearing up out of the mud. I couldn't look. Jack was sobbing. 'I didn't do it – it – it wasn't – m-m-m-my fault . . .'

There was a plunging, sucking noise from the pond and Robert let out a final grunt. Then everything went slack and there was no sound.

I made myself look and saw a shiny, oily mound of black bagpipe dead weight, half out of the water. The rope was around the front legs and had pulled the calf forward onto its knees, throwing its head back.

I could see its chin quite clearly, the tiny, scratchy beginnings of whiskers on its chin, the purple-blue cushion of its out-turned lips, one solitary fly, parading there. And its eyes, its eyelashes, its legs, tangled in river, the little nutty hooves, the soft drum of him, contained in his own pouch, and snot dribbling out of his mouth and nose like the river being wrung out.

Robert had dropped the rope and was stood with his two great hands at his sides as if about to pull guns from holsters and shoot the world. 'Dad's gonna kill me,' he said grimly.

'But it wasn't your fault.' I was looking at Jack who was shaking and snivelling.

'I should have been here – he won't listen.'

Suddenly as if a trap had been lifted, Jack turned and ran.

'You'd better go.' Robert looked up for a second and I caught his eyes full on. At the slightest sign from him I'd have tied myself to his side, but he hung his head and said again, 'Go on, go home.'

'Are you sure?'

'Yes, go!'

Once I had turned, I wanted to be as far from that spot as I could. But I didn't start to run until I'd got over the other side of the bridge. And then, with the duffle bag beating on my back all the way up the hill, I didn't look back.

21

When I got to the cottage I was running again, past the rowan tree, thumping along the flagstones to the kitchen door where I stood winded with the exertion of it.

Amelia and Biddy were at the table, peering round from where they were trying to open another tin of beans.

'Where've you been?'

'Where's Jack?'

'Dunno.'

'Have you seen him?'

'Nope.'

I was panicky, like being on a boat and the waves rising just too friskily. Always before, I'd been able to wind up the stories. We'd played them out by my rules; I was Bobbie, Amelia was Phyllis. The father always came back.

I went upstairs and into the bedroom. My steps sounded hollow; there was no one in there. I took the bag from around my neck and shoved it under the bed, back into the far, dusty corner. Then I jumped from the bedroom step, across the landing to the open door of the living room where I could see the light flickering from the TV. Jack was hunched in Daddy's chair watching, with the sound turned right down.

'Are you OK?' I asked. He didn't answer. I got hold of his arm and pinched him. 'Are you OK?' He still said nothing, hardly squirming. 'Jack, what happened?' He shook his arm free of me with only a trace of protest, but still no words.

It was hard to get to grips with him. Mummy and Daddy sometimes discussed sending him away. He stole, he took money from Mummy's handbag; he lied; he came home from school with huge calculator watches he said he'd been given; he didn't cry; he used to pee in a welly at night to save getting up. I was frightened that he had lost his conscience.

'Jack!'

He didn't flinch.

'Jack!'

He looked at me blankly as if he didn't know who I was.

My voice began to sound like a recording, like it wasn't even coming from my mouth. 'What are you doing? You shouldn't be up here. You should go and tell Mr Burden what happened. It isn't fair, leaving it – What did happen?' My worst fear was that I wouldn't recognise him, that he had been turned into a Midwich Cuckoo. It reminded me of when he was three or four and had hurt himself and held his breath until he fell to the floor. The first time it happened Mummy thought he was dead.

'Well?'

'Bitch,' he muttered under his breath.

I hit him on the back of his head. 'Don't you dare call me that you toerag. Looney Linda! Turn the telly off!'

'Turn it off yourself.' He ran out of the room, out of the front door, slamming it behind him.

'What's the matter with him?' Amelia asked when I got back down.

'God knows.'

She wasn't even stirring the beans in the pan and I could smell them turning to tar. 'Take them off, you thick arse! Can't you see they're burning?'

At five to five when he still hadn't come back, we set off for the phone box without him. I pulled the heavy red-framed door back, and climbed in, hit by the fug of heated air and plastic, then Amelia pushed in, then Biddy.

The door wouldn't close properly. Biddy was half in, half out. She launched herself against us. From the outside, it might have looked like a giant jam jar dipped in a pond, full of all the bits of us, our arms, legs, feet, heads, faces, indistinguishable.

Biddy was wrestling for space, and dug her elbow into Amelia who yelped and shouted at her, 'Get off me, you stink bomb.'

'Keep your voice down,' I hissed. 'Just shut up.'

When the phone went, it was so loud and sudden it made me leap out of my skin. I picked up the receiver quickly to stop it. 'Hello?' I wasn't sure it would be them.

'Hello? Ruth? Hello, darling, how are you?'

I had already decided to tell them nothing. 'Fine.'

'How's Jack?'

'He's fine – Ow! They're all here – Ow! Get off me!'

'Can I say hello?'

I didn't answer but held the receiver above their heads. Amelia reached up and I dropped it so that it hit her shoulder – 'Bitch face!' – and slipped like a kitten, dangling over her back. She twisted round and pulled the cord bringing it back to her ear. 'Mummy? It's me, Amelia.'

I could still hear Mummy's voice, 'How are you? Is Ruth being bossy?'

'Yes, she's being a bitch.'

'Come on darling, just until we get back. Let me talk to Biddy.'

'Bye then.'

Biddy's face lit up. 'Hello, Mummy. Are you having a nice time?'

'Yes, sweetie, are you? Are you OK?'

'Jack stinks!'

'Is he being good?'

'No. He stinks.'

'Can I speak to him?'

'Bye.' She holds out the receiver disdainfully to me, pulling down the corners of her mouth and drops it so that it swings.

'Jack, Jack,' Mummy's voice is like a fly in a matchbox.

I reach down for the handset and bring it back to my ear. 'No, it's Ruth. We've got to go for lunch tomorrow.'

'Is Jack all right?'

'Yes, he's fine. He's gone off to the farm.'

'Don't let him be a nuisance, will you?'

'What can I do about it?'

'Just don't let him be a nuisance. Lunch?'

'At the Burdens.'

'How kind of them. Make sure you say thank you.'

'Of course.'

'Good girl. We'll be back on Monday, in the morning some time. OK?'

'All right. Bye.'

'Bye, then. Make sure you—'

I hooked the receiver back in place, cutting her off. I don't know what I expected from them, but there was a niggling disappointment and emptiness to it. 'Let's get out of here.' I shoved the door by pushing the two of them forward and we tumbled out into the open air. Amelia hit Biddy, 'It!' and ran off into the road. 'Don't go on the road!' I yelled after them, almost crying with the weight of it, the reassertion of bossiness over everything and anything I wanted to be.

GRAHAM

22

Graham was unloading chicken feed from the pick-up when he felt the prickle of being watched. He peered over the sack he was carrying. It was Jack, balancing on one foot, finger in his mouth. 'All right?' Graham said, trying to shift him.

Jack didn't answer and Graham, unnerved by him standing there said, 'What've you been up to, then?'

Still no answer.

Jack was staring at him, at his tight face, which seemed to tighten under his gaze.

'What is it?' There was an edge of irritation about him as he let the sack drop to his feet. 'Shouldn't you be getting back home?'

Jack let his foot unhook from behind his leg and he turned on the spot, looking towards the black mound that lay exposed at the side of the pond.

For a moment Graham was knocked sideways. His mouth hung open. He could have fallen to his knees because of what was entering his head. *Shunt, shunt, shunt*: his brain whirred as whatever it was lying there began to dredge mirror images from the deep recesses of his mind. *Shunt, shunt, shunt*. Putting words to it, to what he saw, was for a sickening moment, too complicated.

He remembered as the boys were growing up how his brother's name would slip out of his mouth by mistake when he was shouting for something to be done, 'Ed!', when he meant to say 'Dan!' or 'Robbie!' It was the same now: a confusion of names.

Eventually what surfaced was Daniel. Two years, almost to the day, he'd gazed in that same place at the sweet crumpled body of his son curled up in the cab, cut loose by firemen like an animal out of a womb. The bright red metal of the cab ripped, jagged as a saw's edge – the indelible stain of oil. The memory so unacceptably new, so sharp, it seemed as if his vision of it would never dry.

They'd taken him away before Alison had arrived back off the bus from Hexham. He'd waited for her, driving the comb he kept in his pocket so hard into the palm of his hand that he broke one of the teeth. When she reached the bridge, the throb of irritation at her delay, the grief that crossed his face made her hesitate before letting the bags drop to her feet.

'What is it?'

He couldn't speak but carried on with the teeth of the comb biting his thumb, looking at her, filling his eyes with her.

She asked again, the bags splurging forward in enquiry disgorging their contents. He was worrying her now and she began to sense that something was wrong, something she might not want to hear and her voice quavered. She watched his brow corrugating. An undistinguishable sound escaped his mouth like a spider.

'Graham, tell me what's happened?' She was trying to see beyond him, peering towards the house.

He looked at her with his mouth hung open, then he turned and she abandoned the shopping, tripping after him, saying, 'Graham, you're frightening me. Please tell me what's wrong?'

He took a deep breath between strides and said leadenly, 'It's Daniel.'

'What's he done?' she said hopefully, relieved almost, thinking he'd been naughty, that he hadn't been pulling his weight.

He couldn't bear to look at her. 'There's no words for it.'

'Graham — what?'

He stopped and turned round to face her, his blear eyes, his jaw crumpling.

'My God — what?'

When he opened his mouth it was like someone leaning over a rail to be sick, the sea rocking. She could taste what he tasted, the foul seaweed in his mouth; the lining of his mouth, seaweed. His head, his hands were shaking.

She couldn't go near, as if she would catch something if she touched him.

'The tractor. He turned it over by the mill. He turned it over on himself — Why would he do that?' he asked in a voice that squeaked at the edges.

Jack was still behind him, but far enough away to be out of reach. How much more could a man take! It got so that he was afraid of himself. Graham spun round, hearing a snivelling. 'Do you know what this is? Do you know what's happened?'

'It wasn't me — It wasn't my fault.'

'Go home. Go on. Go back home!'

As Jack began to run from him, Graham strode over to the animal and in an attempt to pull the situation back to daylight he tapped the creature with the toe of his boot. It seeped foul pond water. 'Have you any idea?' Speaking was only a way of holding back tears of rage or disappointment or failure or grief.

LIZZIE

23

It's only half past nine when she looks at her watch. After the phone call, hearing their voices, so disengaged from her, so separate, she'd felt even more desperate. They'd been and eaten in a pizza place with little waitresses in black tights, tiny skirts, white shirts and ponytails. She feels jaded, the bags under her eyes.

'I'm shattered.' John flings his grey corduroy jacket on the chair and a coin falls to the floor. Lizzie sits against the studded headboard with her knees drawn up. 'It's not late.'

'It's been a long day.'

He continues to undress, placing his boots next to each other by the chair, pulling his shirt over his head without undoing the buttons. He's always been skinny; he hasn't delivered children.

He undoes his belt and climbs out of his trousers, flings them on the same chair, another coin spins on its edge and rolls under the bed.

'It was all right, wasn't it, today?'

'Yes, I think so. Most things done.'

It feels, she thinks, as if she has the lid of a heavy chest open and that the effort of keeping it upright, with the accumulated strength of her whole body, is making her break.

She hugs her knees. 'Do you remember once, you said to me – you said, "I'll love you till your thighs are wrinkled" – do you remember that?'

'What? I don't know – Did I say that?'

'I remember. More than once you said it.' She looks straight at him accusingly. 'I liked it.'

He doesn't answer her and she drops her head again, glaring down at her bare toes, rocking forwards against her drawn-up thighs. 'How're you feeling, then – now?'

'All right,' he answers, nervously. 'I'm all right.'

He makes the mistake however of leaving it there and she is filled instantaneously with howling misery. *What about me?* She hunches further up the bed and breathes hard.

'Have you spoken to her? Have you really finished it? Is it over, really over?' she asks as levelly as she can. She has never asked anything quite so direct before and he is disarmed.

'Yes, it is.'

'When?'

'It's over. I said it was. That's all.'

She feels the reprimand; and the smarting is enough to uncheck her fury. 'But I *need* to know. I wish I'd never needed to know anything, that you'd fucking never given me any cause to ever know anything!' She is up on her knees and the bed is bobbing as she emphasises what she is saying with her arm. The words in her mouth are silting up, choking her. 'Why did you do this to me?'

He is hanging his head, and he says, out of habit, to get the last word: 'I'm not the only one.'

'What?'

He sighs as if it's her that is pulling this out of him. 'What about Marcus Whatsit, turning up the other day? What was he after?'

'Nothing!' She is incredulous, but at the same time registers the flicker of his suspicion as a positive sign.

'What was he doing, then?'

'He wasn't *doing* anything. People come and go – that's life. He came; he went.'

'And there's poets – how many of them do we hear about? The Russian the other day, the ever-so-sensitive Cruickshank—'

'You're pathetic! It's a class. I'm learning how to do something – I'm finally getting some sort of a life.'

'Right!'

'How dare you use that. I've done absolutely nothing. Why should I be happy to be left cooking, cleaning, mopping up after everyone? Why should you begrudge me when I find something to do with my life that makes me feel alive? *She* gets out, doesn't she? *She* gets around. You're the one that's having an affair, for God's sake.'

'Maybe it was only a matter of time.'

'You can't say that. I loved you. I do love you. You know I do.'

'It's too easy to say. It doesn't mean anything, to say it.'

'What do you want? Blood? Shall I slit my wrists?'

'You always do this. I don't want a scene. I'm tired. I just want to sleep.'

'How can you sleep? I can't sleep. I haven't slept for months.'

'Don't exaggerate.'

'What about the children? Have you thought for one minute what it's doing to them? You seem to think they're not your responsibility, that you can walk away and sweep back in whenever you feel like it.'

'Don't be ridiculous, of course I care about them.'

'You don't even notice. Why do you think Biddy went off? Why do you think Jack can't read?'

'It's got nothing to do with it.'

'It's got everything to do with it – you're blind, you're completely blind to it. She's taken your eyes, she's taken your brain.'

'I'm around for them.'

'They won't want anything to do with you, when they know.'

'They don't need to *know* anything.'

'They're not stupid, of course they know.'

She is wrung out with nowhere to go and her mind rattles around like a pinball in her head bashing at anything that will make him comprehend. She lights on his jacket. 'I want the keys.'

He's not answering her, lying where he's crept between the yellow nylon sheets of his bed, which are drawn tightly around him like stockings. His voice is muffled, 'You can't drive, you've drunk too much.'

'I don't give a shit. Give me the keys. I don't believe you. I can never believe you now and I can't bear to be in the same room as you. You make me sick, you filthy, lying bastard. Give me the keys!'

He fishes his glasses off and puts them onto the bedside table, ducks his head down and draws his legs up protectively.

'Where are they?' She lunges for his jacket and begins shaking it upside down onto the floor. He lifts his head and rips himself out of the bed, bringing the sheets with him.

'Don't be so bloody stupid – leave that alone!'

The keys fall out with coins and a confetti of torn-up tickets and he grabs the bunch and holds them to him, crouched around them. She flares, hitting at him, pummelling his back with her fists, as hard as she can. 'You fucking bastard!'

He is rigid, hunched like a giant turtle. His skin prickles all over with sweat. She falls back onto her own bed and draws her feet up, backing up against the headboard. She can feel the edge of it in her neck as she hits out at the wall behind with the back of her head, hard, hard, hard. However much she hammers, the hurt is out; it runs amok and won't be put away, dancing naked, laughing at her, smeared in war paint, a penis that dances and swings, reaching in all directions as if it's having the time of its life.

RUTH

24

I couldn't sleep. First of all there was the whole palaver of investigating the ghost. There was a noise, a humming noise that came and went, from downstairs. Amelia was getting Biddy hysterical and she was cramming her mouth with the edge of her sleeping bag, about to make herself sick.

'I'll go!'

I got halfway down the stairs and the noise began again; I charged back up, laughing but not in a very convincing way, suddenly letting myself believe that perhaps it was true. Like Grandmother's footsteps. 'See,' Amelia said veneomously, 'you didn't believe us. Now who's the scared one?'

'It's not a ghost. Don't be stupid. There aren't ghosts. You can't still believe in ghosts.'

'I don't,' Jack yells from the bottom of his sleeping bag.

'No one does.'

'What is it then?'

'It's probably just the stream that goes under the floor.'

'Well, why don't you go down there, then? Prove it. Prove there's nothing there!'

'OK then, OK I will.'

I set out again and the two of them followed me to the top of the stairs. It was like climbing down a masthead, slowly, slowly, so that

I didn't lose my balance, the walls flaking against my hands, the stairs creaking like sails.

Cyril had told Mummy how the two sisters had ended up sharing the downstairs room even though the floor had caved in right in the middle and there was a drop of at least ten feet to where the stream flowed underneath. They had to make their way around the edges of the room to the two chairs over by the window. No one knows when they started fighting. In the end one had brought the other a glass of water and the other had taken it off her and instead of thanking her had begun flicking the water at her sister as she sat down to pick up the knitting beside her. The sister had ignored her until finally the one with the water had taken what was left in the cup and thrown it in the other's face. Then she had gone upstairs without a word and locked herself in her room for a week; the other one stayed downstairs, refusing to budge, even to go to bed.

When we moved in, for the first few years the room was kept locked so we couldn't go and fall down the hole. Then Mr Docker had come and filled the floor with concrete, using rubble that he was conveniently digging up for someone from the old school playground across the valley. Right from when it was a room again none of us had ever wanted to sleep in there and it ended up getting more and more cluttered with bits and pieces of rescued furniture from the dump.

Halfway down the stairs the humming began again and I froze. Amelia and Biddy shrieked and vanished inside the bedroom. I didn't dare turn to climb the stairs but felt my way up backwards, hardly drawing breath and slammed the bedroom door behind me.

Hours later, I was still awake. It was weirdly light as if the moon contained an electric bulb. I listened for ages to the alternate exhalations of Amelia and Biddy, thinking that all would be well as long as we stayed put.

Suddenly, from the corner, there was a different, active sound. There were mice in the cottage – we'd seen one earlier that week, popping its head up like a joke out of the fireplace – and automatically I stiffened, shut my mouth tight. The sound bodied out to become a figure stirring and my first instinct was panic, for being the one who'd have to deal with it.

Seconds later I'd woken up enough to recognise the outline, the fist of Jack's head. He was moving about with all his clothes on like a burglar. I kept still and watched as he padded exaggeratedly over Biddy's mattress and leant his whole body against the door, to ease up the latch, releasing it over its crook so quietly, like cracking a safe.

I was properly awake now and thinking only that I had to follow him, to keep track of him; there was a purposefulness about his movements that worried me. He was up to no good, or going to light a fire somewhere that would burn us all up. I crept towards the door in the uphill and downhill of the breathing that filled the room. When I got to the landing he was already beyond the bottom of the stairs inside the kitchen. On his own! He must have forgotten about the ghosts. Perhaps he'd gone to get a drink? Perhaps he was only being furtive out of habit?

Halfway down, the click of a switch underneath me lit the joints of the treads like a staircase to heaven. He was underneath, in the pantry. I trod at the very edge of each step, feeding my hands flat over each other against the wall. When I got to the kitchen door, I was less careful, finding myself right next to the room with Mr Burden's aunts. It was freezing under my feet and I wanted to get to him, to prove quickly to myself that it *was* him and not a spectre got up to lure me downstairs. I made for the glow that outlined the door and pulled at it so suddenly that light fell like a bucket of water over me.

Jack was sitting on a low stool, cowering. He was a strange grey colour under the bare bulb, his hand poised like a paw, grubby. He had the half-empty bowl of a rice pudding, which also had a greenish tinge, propped on his knee and had been scooping at it, cramming the rubbery rice into his mouth.

He was hunching his shoulders cravenly as if I was going to beat him, as if I was a monster and would screech and reveal him to the whole house. His look surprised and disarmed me: instantly I felt sorry for him and guilty for ever having given him cause to mistrust me.

His mouth closed around what was in it but he didn't swallow.

I used to feed him his puddings when he was a baby, so that I could eat two spoonfuls of chocolate mousse for every one he ate. He was sweet then, with long curly hair just like a girl. Then so quickly he'd become like all of us, fighting his own corner, not giving an inch to the others.

'What are you doing?'

He looked straight ahead, his lips drawn in so that they no longer showed.

'It's all right, I won't tell — I do that, sometimes, you know. That's my trick.'

Still he didn't move, but shuddered involuntarily.

'Why don't you go back to bed? Save the rest for tomorrow – It's cold down here.'

He let me take the bowl out of his hands without stirring. I opened the door of the ancient, heavy fridge and immediately it began to hum.

'Jack! It was the fridge! It was the fridge all along! Weren't they scaredy-cats! It was just the fridge making that humming noise.'

'Why did it come out dead?' he asked, shivering. 'When Robert pulled him out? Why was it dead?'

'Because it drowned. It couldn't swim.'

'But before when we pulled it out it was fine.'

'It's not the same. It had to breathe. It only had water to breathe.'

'I didn't do it! It didn't listen to me. I said stop it. I said stop it all the way.'

'Come on. I know you did. It's not your fault. Come on. They'll be back soon.'

I held my hand out and took his sticky fingers stiffly into mine, pulling him from the stool. 'Come on. Let's go back to bed.'

I wished then that I'd been able to give in and put my arms around him, squeeze him and all the sadness that I could feel bubbling up in him. I knew that that's what would have been right; it would have happened like that in a film. But I just couldn't. There was something in us all like soldiers. We didn't touch. It was the most I could do to take his hand.

LIZZIE

25

She wonders if there could be anything worse than waking in a B & B, that a ditch would be preferable. At least then you didn't have to have the breakfast. You didn't have to face those anonymous others who had spent the night in adjacent rooms and probably heard everything and wondered what the hell was going on and putting voices to faces. No one could accuse you out loud of ruining their night or bringing their B & B into disrepute because you were paying for it, and you would be gone after breakfast, but you could see them thinking it, or that there must be something unforgivable about her, something that would let a man let a woman beat her head against the wall until all the lights in the place, including the timed light on the landing last thing went out.

Lizzie felt her eyes were two ash holes in the snow, her skin so melted that she couldn't bear to look. Her hair was string and she pulled it back. Words had stopped carrying anything for her; they tinkled like bits of tin. Rain was half-hearted at the window. It felt cold in the room and she shivered. Shivering reminded her of crying.

John was up. He hadn't bothered washing. 'We'd better go down.'

She shrugged in agreement and made for the door. There was no way they could avoid the breakfast. Mrs whatever would be unavailable to take their money, cooking away in the kitchen, the full works. They sloped down the stairs and into the dark dining room. There was a heavy sideboard with packets of cereal and tinned grapefruit laid out in bowls. There were three tables of two in the room, one occupied by a middle-aged couple, who looked up briefly as they came in. They weren't talking, but continued a mute conversation they were having that involved swapping the food on their plates. She had his egg, he took her black pudding and sausage.

John and Lizzie pulled the chairs out from the farthest table and sat down. John coughed into his sleeve.

The woman came out with an apron tied around her waist. 'Tea or coffee?'

'Coffee, please'

'Yes, coffee for me, too.'

'You'll help yourself to cereal on the sideboard there.'

'Thank you.'

'Full breakfast?'

'Could I just have egg and mushrooms, please?'

'I'll have the lot, thanks.' John handed her back the folded menu.

She seemed about to add something, but thought better of it and licked her pencil. 'That's it, then.' The small talk, the stuff about a nice night's sleep and the room being comfortable, in this case, she thought best left unsaid.

When it came, it astounded Lizzie that he was able to eat. She wished she'd said she'd been on a diet. The mushrooms and egg seemed to decompose in her mouth. She hid what she could under a slice of toast. Before they left she couldn't help herself taking two extra miniature pots of tartan jam for Biddy and for Jack.

RUTH

26

I didn't know what to do about lunch. Perhaps we'd be expected not to go? But it was too rude not to turn up, if we'd been asked. We hadn't been un-asked.

As soon as I mention it, Jack shakes his head and I can see that there's no point in trying to persuade him.

'Why's Jack not coming?' Biddy asks.

'It doesn't matter.'

Amelia and Biddy are oblivious. They clatter off down the lane with me trying to keep up: I don't want to be the first there, but I don't want to be the last either. Amelia goes straight up to the back door. No one answers for a bit and I begin to think this is the best outcome: that we've tried and now we can go home. But the door opens like a trap door and Mrs Burden appears looking anxious.

Biddy and Amelia are standing boot-faced, presenting themselves.

'Come in. Is that all of you? Come inside. Where's Jack?'

'He wanted to stay behind.'

'Is he all right?' she asks.

'Yes, he's fine, he doesn't really like Sunday lunch – he doesn't eat meat.'

'You're sure he'll be all right?'

'He's watching telly.'

It is so much darker in the kitchen than outside and maybe it is just that, making the room feel shut down. Robert is at the table, nursing a can of something, his leg jiggling up and down; he raises his head briefly but doesn't meet my eye. Mr Burden has his back to us by the sideboard, his shirt sleeves rolled up and his hair combed wet and dark against his neck. He is sharpening a knife vigorously and doesn't turn round.

'Sit down.' Mrs Burden motions to the chairs at the table, holding onto the back of one as if it was a person. 'Ruth, why don't you go next to me – Amelia, that's right, next to Robert – that's it.'

She brings a china dish to the table in a cloth and the lid clatters with a terrible noise as she puts it down. Mr Burden is picking over the meat and distributing a brown pile on each plate, which she ferries for him to the table. I watch for the inevitable turn of Biddy's face, as if she's being handed poison. 'Help yourself to carrots and potatoes.'

Amelia looks around and shrugs, takes the spoon and wades into the carrots. A potato is set loose, rolling across the table, over the edge, a little splut as it lands open on the floor. She smirks in apology as if she's at school and then begins to spoon carrots onto Biddy's plate, knowing she won't eat them and I watch helplessly as Biddy begins to fork them back into the dish, one by one.

Mr Burden flumps down and coughs into his fist. Then he lifts his chin up to the ceiling. 'For what we are about to receive . . .'

Biddy has already started to eat and I try to reach her under the table. She stalls and spits out what's in her mouth.

Mr Burden clears his throat irritably, '. . . may the Lord make us truly thankful. Amen.'

I can feel Mrs Burden right up against me clenching her knife and fork. She takes a deep breath. 'How're you getting on?' she asks.

'Fine. Fine,' I say, nodding perhaps too emphatically.

Then there is nothing, a desert, with just the scrape of cutlery on china and the churning of food, and I can almost feel the spikes growing out of me and towards me like a hothouse full of cacti.

'When are they back?' Mr Burden asks eventually, depositing a forkful into his mouth.

'Tomorrow. Sometime after lunch, I think.'

He removes a thread of meat from his tooth with a fingernail. 'What are they doing up there, anyway?'

I feel myself buckle under the load of keeping things going, Amelia and Biddy as usual feeling no obligation to help me out.

'They go to galleries, to bookshops and things.'

He raises his eyes.

Out of nowhere, like a rabbit out of a hat, Robert belches. Biddy catches her breath in delight and then all of a sudden she gasps and her eyes start; she chokes out the contents of her mouth.

'Robert!' Mrs Burden sounds horrified. She bends forwards across the table to Biddy. 'Are you all right? Would you like some water?'

Biddy looks bruised in the face and pushes herself back from the table, shaking her head. *Don't do this!* I am transfixed by the unbearableness of it.

'That's it – you're all right now, aren't you?' Mrs Burden is saying, but she is craned forward anxiously, ready to leap out of her chair.

'Do your mother and father often leave you like this?' Mr Burden asks. 'How old are you?'

'I'm sixteen soon,' I say it weakly, intensely aware of Robert, who seems determined to avoid me, shifting the food around on his plate, tipping his head back to take the can of lager.

'Robert, use a glass!'

He leans back languidly on two legs of his chair and reaches for the cupboard under the dresser. He brings out a tumbler and pours the jewel-like liquid sleepily from a height so that it froths up and over the rim. He moves forward with his lips as if he is going to kiss it, leaving a print of bubbles under his nose.

'Don't monkey about!' Mr Burden thumps the table and the plates give a little skip in their places. 'Where'd you get that stuff from, anyway?'

It is only then that it occurs to me that we've been playing a game, a memory game. All the objects neatly on a tray: the kitchen sink, the table, the chairs, the cutlery, Mrs Burden, Mr Burden, Robert. And something, someone missing.

We have an old print of *Balthazar's Feast* in our bedroom that has been there as long as I can remember. Did Daddy once tell me the story? Enough, anyway for me to recognise the blinding flash of writing on the wall.

Even the room has not forgotten and it is suddenly brilliantly clear that the people in the room have not forgotten either: Daniel, between them, erupting from the gloom like a puppy that has been shut out all night.

Mr Burden is at the end of his tether. 'Come on. Don't play silly buggers!'

'You'll have to excuse me a second,' Mrs Burden mumbles, getting up hastily, nudging my elbow, and she disappears through the pantry door leaving behind a ghost of herself in the room.

ALISON

27

Only the boys and Graham ever used the downstairs lavatory. Through the pantry, along the corridor that was once an outside yard, roofed over in the sixties with a sheet of corrugated plastic, and now dark with the accumulation of leaves and impossible-to-get-at mould. The door has warped so that it doesn't shut properly; she'd never send visitors out there. Alison pulls it back. There's only standing room. The seat is up and the bowl, cracked and yellow. There is the thinnest light from a head-high, book-sized window and from what little filters through the plastic roof; it's just possible to see the shadow of a brown tidemark on the water line and little globs along the rim. It revolts her against them.

She brings the lid down balancing the edge with the tip of her finger and lets it bang into place. Then she sits down, bent double, holding onto the fronts of her legs just below the knee.

Out of the pocket of her overall she brings a little brown bottle, which she keeps topped up with sherry, for emergencies. She fumbles with the screw top and then tips two mouthfuls of the liquid back to soothe the turmoil of her insides.

The drink in her brain is a mouse behind the skirting, doing its work, finding the cogs, sorting them. She remembers those first mornings after the accident when she'd woken in a panic feeling that the bed was being pulled from under her; that, like a snow plough, time itself was overtaking her, pushing her aside, burying her in the white noise of what stormed in her head. The next day and the next when she got up to go to the bathroom she felt dizzy and had to sit on the landing with her head between her knees. It was as if the person she was, the person who moved about the house, who shut up the chickens, had fallen off its hanger and left a jangling of empty metal in the wardrobe.

After a week there was a pile on her tongue like a carpet and her head was clearly divided: the mouth where things came out and the balcony of her eyes where things entered in. Upstairs and downstairs.

The walls pressed in on her as if she was sitting at the bottom of a dank well. There was a trickling above her head from the cistern, constantly filling itself. *Ding dong bell,* it tinkled, *Pussy's in the well,* like a child's tinny, uneven musical box. *Who put her in? Little Johnny Green!*

The gloom was opaque so that her eyes might have been open or shut. *What a naughty boy was that to try to drown poor pussy cat, who never did any harm.* Her teeth were clenched like pegs on a line. Everything was blowing around in her head until she'd lost all sense of the chronology of things. Was it only yesterday that Graham had burst into the house?

'Where is he?'

'What is it?' She had stubbed out her cigarette automatically, guiltily.

'Where is he?'

'Who?'

'Robert! Robert! Who d'you think, woman? I can't leave the place for one minute and this happens. Didn't you see what was going on?'

'What's happened? I've been upstairs, tidying upstairs, I've just this minute come down. I don't think he's here.'

'He's got no business being out. Leaving things. It's about time he took some responsibility for the place.'

He had looked at her then as if he hated her, as if he'd never made her pay for what she had done.

'Wake up! See for yourself. Go on. Haven't you been outdoors? Go out and see for yourself.'

Woman was so unlike him. It reminded her of his father. She'd snatched at the cigarettes from the table as if she might be leaving home for good. He'd never been violent towards her, but if she hadn't come that second to see what was out there, she felt he'd have dragged her by her hair. He was close behind her, shooing her into the yard, listening to the sound of her stopping; he wasn't going to spare her this time . . .

'*See?*'

By the way her shoulders were hunched he could tell she was recoiling from the sodden creature. All this time he'd protected her, defended her, carrying the weight of everything himself, never saying a word. There was a sense of justness and of deliverance now in putting her face to it, in making her take on board all that he'd taken upon himself from the moment he'd clapped eyes on her. He looked at the bow in her back – he knew – imagined the crack in the blue of her eyes, her drained skin, her body giving way under his hands, her flutter, her quavering, 'I do'; he knew. Her shut mouth. Her closed ears.

Her little boys. So many times, as soon as they could put one foot in front of the other, first Robert, then Daniel, they'd been determined to head for the river, to bury themselves in the river and she'd almost wanted to tie them to a chair or the kitchen table, so they couldn't escape. Even when they'd learned to swim, she still thought the river would trick them away.

Now she couldn't bear to take in what she saw in front of her: the irrefutable length, breadth and weight of a body: the body of the son she hadn't been allowed to see before they'd taken him away: the impossible difference between what she could allow herself to imagine, and what wormed its way into her head, packed so tightly, so combustively that she daren't move an inch.

29

S he slipped back into the room, and laid the oven cloth in her lap. 'Pudding?' she asked in a small voice, looking round, conscious of keeping her breath to herself.

But the silence she had walked into seemed unnegotiable. Graham was rocking in his chair, ready to jump into the abyss, holding hard onto the edge of the table.

'I *love* puddings,' Biddy burbled.

Ruth said, 'I- I think maybe we should go. Thank you. Thank you very much. It was really lovely. Biddy!'

Graham was already on his feet but not able to stand upright, clasping the napkin to his thighs to let her by; Robert, burning to the roots of his hair. Alison got up startled, but grateful for the precipitate conclusion of the meal she had begun to think would never end. She held her hands around their shoulders as if she was dressing them in invisible coats, pushing them out. 'Watch the road.'

They could hear the three children stuttering out of the yard, Amelia in a loud voice whooping, 'We didn't even have to do the washing-up!'

As soon as Alison shut the door on them, Graham boiled over.

'How on earth did they end up coming round here? What're their parents doing letting them run wild over the country?'

'I didn't have any choice,' she said faltering and unprepared.

'You shouldn't have been put in that position. And I shouldn't have to speak to you about manners,' he said, nodding roughly at Robert. 'And take that blasted jacket off. No need to wear it inside, at the table.' Robert sat pushed back in his chair with his legs stretched ahead of him looking down at his hands, chewing his tongue. It was too late, but Graham regretted letting him keep his brother's jacket. Robert had dug it out of the trunk and gleefully appropriated it, wearing it ever since even in blazing sunshine. And then the old bike: he had made it seem a logical progression, rescuing it from the shed, taking it into the shop in Hexham where they'd helped him strip it down, do it up.

Someone must have said something to him about his uncle then, Alison thought. The last few months he'd started asking questions, persistently, where he'd lived, what had happened to him. It irritated Graham. 'What are you talking about? What's Ed got to do with anything now?'

He seemed to bring it out as a way of needling his father, choosing his moments. After the children had gone and Alison was at the sink washing-up, the two of them were left at the table.

'I'm just asking. I'm interested.'

'What's brought this on? Why are you asking?'

'I've heard things, that's all.'

'Who've you been talking to?'

'It doesn't matter.'

'No one's got any business talking about what goes on in this house.'

'It is my business. It's my family, isn't it?'

'If you know so much, why are you asking?'

'I want to hear it from you.'

'What?'

'Is it true?'

'What?'

'Is it true what he did?'

Graham is puce-coloured, sucking in his cheeks. 'What've you been told?' He was trapped and he could see that there was no way out of it but bluster and lies. He felt his chest constrict around the words, 'There isn't anything to tell.'

'Why does everyone else seem to know?'

'Who's everyone else?' Graham looked at him, panicking. But it was impossible to second-guess him. He sucked his lips in harder. 'Don't play games with me.'

'I'm not the one playing games.'

Alison felt herself freeze, holding on to the rim of the sink like she used to do in the swimming pool, terrified of the man with the great pole who'd unlock her arms from the edge.

'I just want to know the truth.'

'Leave it alone. There's been enough upset in this house. For the last time, I'm telling you to leave it.'

RUTH

30

As soon as we were through the yard I grabbed Biddy's hand and squeezed the bones to stop the torrent of mortification and disappointment. 'Get off!' she squealed.

'Shut up! Just shut up and keep going.'

At the top of the hill, Biddy wrenched her hand from mine and stuck out her tongue, following Amelia over the gate into the bull field where they had pitched their house. I stood wavering, sickened by their unbelievable lack of comprehension and exhausted by the effort of even thinking up a way of telling them I didn't give a toss about their pathetic games, without them thinking that I sounded as if I did.

Robert's face plagued me. One minute it had seemed so simple to read and the next he was more aloof than ever, as if I was a baby like Jack. But the further off he took himself, the more I felt it might be a test, that I was bound to him, and had in some way to persevere and to save him. Perhaps he'd taken all the blame and was angry with me? I'd behaved like a coward and said nothing. Maybe he would look at me differently if I went back and told his father what had happened: that it wasn't his fault or Jack's fault or anybody's fault.

I imagined a scenario where the three of them would separately melt around me, Robert smiling his big smile because he knew I'd come through, Mr Burden saying it was good of me to make things clear and Mrs Burden looking on us with her eyes brimming up because she'd wanted it all along to be a happy ending. She wanted more than anything for her son to be happy.

But it wasn't as simple as *Jackie* made out. As quickly as I summoned the photofits, the clinch of cheekbones, the bubbles of celebration, I demolished them with acid scorn: nothing had happened, had it? What on earth did I think had happened? We hadn't even held hands. I was so incensed at myself for having no idea how to proceed that without thinking it through or wondering what I might face when I got there, I forced myself to go back down the hill.

When I got to the farmyard, I moved more cautiously. It was like entering a different atmosphere, browner, thicker air. There was a rumble of voices coming from the open kitchen window and the pitch of them made me hesitate. Then it was as if a stone hurtled out past my shoulder, Mr Burden's voice barking, 'You just don't know when to leave things, do you . . . I'll have no truck with them. I've told you before, her mother is a whoo-er!' And although the window was wide open, it felt as if the glass in the frame had been shattered.

It took a while for the word to fathom the bottom of me, translating itself, spelling itself: *whore!* My mouth drained like the tide being sucked right out. I heard Robert then, quieter, 'You'd know all about that, wouldn't you?'

'I'm your father!'

'You think so?'

'I'm your father!'

'Say it again, you might even believe it!'

'Don't talk to me like that. Who do you think I am?'

Tables and chairs were scraping, as someone barged past. 'You dare speak to me like that in my house! How dare you? I've told you, and I'll tell you again, you can see it in her eyes: any man, he's fair game!'

'Listen to yourself!'

'No one tells me what to do.'

'What's this got to do with anything?'

'Don't you dare bring your mother into this.'

'You're unbelievable.'

'Where are you going? Tell me where you're going. What're you doing?' Mrs Burden's voice, panicked and pleading, 'Go with him, Graham, make sure he doesn't hurt himself . . . please!'

I couldn't move. I heard footsteps going heavily up the stairs and still I couldn't shift, waiting, mesmerised. I thought it was only our family that had rows. It shocked me, hearing Mrs Burden whimpering. It shocked me because I thought it was only us; that even if terrible things happened, other people were normal about it, grown-up. Then the same steps came chundering down; Robert burst out of the front door swinging a green army surplus bag. He went straight to the shed, fixed the bag on the bike and then heaved it off its prop, pushed it outside and swung his leg over, metal chinking in his pockets and his trousers squeaking against the seat. Then he revved and revved and revved like the Leader of the Pack, and let himself go, swerving over the bridge up the hill – a defiant *blare, blare, blare* of his horn – so sudden that when the dust settled, it was as if he'd disappeared into thin air.

ALISON

31

BEEP! BEEP! BEEP! The horn sounded in the kitchen so defiantly and violently that it could have dislodged plates from the dresser. Alison put her hand out to catch the drop she felt about to fall from her nostril, the liquid coming away in her hands, running between her fingers to two bright red splashes on the front of her overall like a tap dripping red ink. Graham was sitting at the table impassively, his hands laid out in front of him, turned upwards. The blood was slippery and wouldn't stop. She led herself by the nose out of the room, stumbling upstairs – not into their own bedroom, where he might come and find her, but to the boys'. She sat down on Daniel's bed and leant forward hearing the blood clicking in her nose between the press of her fingers . . .

The car had appeared from nowhere. It had beeped right beside her, on the wrong side of the road, making her jump, and she'd recognised the face, with the window wound down, leaning towards her . . .

'Where are you off to? Need a lift?'

She was flummoxed. 'I'm going home. Working nights – I'm off home.'

'Do you want a ride?'

'It's no distance, really.'

Alison had been feeling dead on her feet and numb from the

demands of an old man and his bedpan and the loneliness of being the only hale person awake on the ward at three in the morning. He could see her faltering.

'Come on . . . I'll take you for a little spin, if you like? What've you got to get back to?' From his side he fumbled with the passenger door and pushed it out towards her. 'Go on, hop in. Live dangerously!'

She looked out from the collar of her cape, up and down the street. There was no one around. Her heart was pounding.

'Come on. Father's let me out with the car. The world's my oyster. Long as I get it back in one piece.'

She smiled at him and in one spur of the moment move gathered and folded herself into the front seat, pulled shut the door and set her bag on her knee.

'Fancy meeting you here. Let me show you what she can do.' He revved the engine more violently than was needed and put the car in gear, taking off so that she was flattened to her seat.

'How's it going – Oxford?' Alison asked tentatively, and the word itself made her think of a place like heaven, beautifully coordinated like the golden insides of a perfectly balanced pocket watch.

'Oh, it's all right – busy, lots to do, lots of people.'

'It must seem quiet to you, strange, coming back here.'

'I quite like it, really. Bit of peace. Recharge my batteries.'

Their two pairs of legs were dark in the wells below the dashboard, his hand, from the corner of her eye, moving out from the cuff of his jacket, over and around the gear stick, the dark fine hairs on the backs of his wrists.

'How's Eileen behaving?' He looked round and caught her eye.

'Fine,' Alison said, as if she was complicit in something.

'Sure she is,' he said. 'So, what shall we do? Where shall we go?'

'I'd be back at the home, usually, sleeping.'

'What a waste of a day. Lucky I caught you.'

There was a sort of delirium to that early hour, the empty streets. From the moment he'd pulled up, tiredness had evaporated or the ability to detect tiredness, or to care. Being driven in a car was novelty enough, but in a car driven by the boy who'd got a scholarship to Oxford, out of all the school, out of the whole of Hexham . . .

There was a photograph of him that Eileen kept on the dressing table in their bedroom, his long black gown, trying not to smile. It was as if they shared that photograph. And once Alison had met him for herself, there was no end to Eileen's mentioning of him, the array of jobs he might do when he left.

From the very first his presence had had a strange effect on Alison, a fascination, like water over sand. He was a creature from another planet altogether, from a zoo, from different air. She never told Eileen, but in her head, she'd begun to see him like Heathcliffe, like someone without a family at all, a type of new being. She couldn't help wondering what life with a man like that would be. And now she was being driven out of town by him; it was the unimaginable fulfilment of a wish that she could hardly dared to have hoped for.

He was smiling at her like he was checking up in short bursts every now and again. She was itching to take her cap off, but waited until they were out of town. Then she moved her bag next to her feet and began fishing for the pins in her hair, bringing the stiff white cap down to fiddle with in her lap. Her heart bobbed very close to the surface, and she was aware for the first time in her life of living only on the wave of the present, right at its very edge.

There was an exhilaration to it, as if the very fact that she was removed from solid ground, moving and not still, lifted her from who she was; as if she could reconstitute herself, cell by cell as they went along, the simple governing impulse being proximity to him, like any husband and wife, out for a drive, and a wilful longing for it not to end.

With one hand on the steering wheel he felt with his left hand in the pocket of his jacket, and drew out, without looking, a bottle, offering it to her. 'Go on. Good for the cold.'

Alison took it unquestioningly, unscrewed the top and sipped clumsily, burning her lips, her tongue numb, the sharp evaporation of liquid on her breath.

'Are you going to stick the nursing? Not sure Eileen will.'

'I hadn't thought – it's a good job. I like it.'

'Don't tell her I said so.'

'No, of course, I won't.'

'I think she's after a doctor and early retirement.'

Alison giggled uncharacteristically and lifted her legs from the floor, turning down her heels.

The day had begun with a red sky and frost, but had given way to dense pearly fog and the threat of rain or snow. She hadn't been concentrating on where they were driving. The only sign she'd been aware of was at Burnhope; then they'd turned off along the back roads, sometimes straight, sometimes winding. The speed was infectious; it made her heart thump.

'Have you ever been to a race?' he asked her suddenly as they began climbing a steep hill. 'Ever been up here?'

'Where are we?'

'The racecourse! Have you never been? The view's amazing up here on a good day. Come on, I'll show you. It's freezing now, but in the spring it's the best place. We'll have to fix that. Perhaps when I next come down . . .'

She was radiant at the thought of it. Racing had the ring of something exciting and forbidden, and he was already mentioning another time, and his coming back; and to her.

As they got up onto the tops she could make out the pavilions and wooden huts of the racecourse. 'Hard to believe it now, but on a clear day you can see for miles.'

Today they were cocooned in grey. And from the grey distance, there were definite signs of something breaking off, floating towards them, just one or two snatches at first blowing down on them like feathers or ash. He leaned forward and up over the wheel. 'Bugger! If this picks up I'm going to have to pull off the road. The wipers aren't good: we'll not be able to see straight in this stuff.'

Alison peered out with him and something made her will it on, like a chorus of angels, it was the sort of snow that could appear all of a sudden, taking hold of the sky like a swarm.

'Sorry about this,' he said. 'I'm going to have to turn off here, all right? Just till it clears; till it packs up.'

He drew into a gateway and pulled up the handbrake. When the engine stopped there was no sound at all. 'Well,' he said, 'we'll just have to twiddle our thumbs for a bit.'

The inside of the windscreen was obscured with condensation and outside the snow was like a veil being drawn. He turned purposefully to face her, pulling his knee up onto the seat. 'Cold out here, isn't it?' And then he added, with a grin, 'You're a nurse: what's the best way you know to keep warm?' His head was to one side, hands at his waist. When she hesitated, he raised them like a showman, and quickly, before she had a moment to think, he moved towards her, encircling her so she could feel the tiny black hairs on the tip of his nose. She didn't mean to, but she flinched.

'It's all right. I won't bite.'

'No – I didn't think . . .'

'Come here then . . .'

He took her chin and pulled her face to meet his. Alison's mouth was shut; she'd never been kissed before. She caved in. He smelt of burning honey, she thought, and of bees.

He had his arm around the side of her head pulling her to him and then with one finger brushed the top of her forehead, which like an open sesame rolled away her sense of what or what not to do. The outside world was blind, and she was anyone but herself, light as eggwhite, folding in her lot with him, involved now in a mesmerising rearrangement of limbs that brought her lying almost straight out beside him, head beneath the steering wheel, like a fork, his back at a right angle to her, flat against the squeaky maroon upholstery. He held her in place by the urgency of his look, held her by the eye, so she was concentrating on its glassy reflections, ignoring the cold air she could feel climbing up her thigh and the fumbling there.

'You're so soft, aren't you?' he mumbled, his hands pressing her as if he was making her, shaping her again out of clay. And then he grasped her hand and brought it towards him, placed it over the front of his trousers. 'You've done that,' he whispered. 'Look what you've done!'

And with her hand still there, he unlatched his belt, worked the buttons of his fly. There was no way back but to go on with what she had started. She had got him here and it was too late to change her mind. She looked at him intently, entrusting her being to him like she'd hand over a sick child.

She could feel the tug of her skirt, pulling her towards him, and then as he prodded and poked and beat a path into the tiny chink of her, and as he gasped and his eyes flitted from her to above the dials on the dashboard, and blank, blank, blank, he dealt her a grave and expanding pain, she panicked, finding herself pressed flat by an utter lack of recognition, and a bull's weight, a ridiculous ungainliness and ugliness about how she was lying with the handbrake digging into her spine, almost collapsing off the seat into the well of the car.

Alison's heart was dead in her mouth. It could have been an ice age, an iron age and yet it was no time at all. For a moment he held himself in place on top of her as if sorting out his best move, then he pulled away and back. He was dishevelled in his face as he smoothed back the lick of his hair. His breath flung out the smell of drink like a net, suddenly making her gag. 'All right?' he said, shuffling further back on his seat and beginning to tuck his shirt into his trousers, finding the hole for the needle of his belt. He was looking out again as he did it, making a round hole in the condensation with the back of his hand. 'Not so bad now, we might risk it in a minute.'

She wanted to grab onto him, even though it was clear the day had stopped, because it seemed the only conceivable way to keep things going, preserving a moment that was otherwise crumbling and caving in under her feet.

'Johnny?' It was the first time she'd ever used his name out loud. 'Yep?'

But she could see he wasn't going to listen. Already he had the door half open and was bending his head to get out, wiping snow vigorously from the windscreen with his sleeve. He came back inside, sitting down heavily, lifting in his feet one by one, slamming the door. 'Well? We should get going.'

When she said nothing he looked round. 'All right?' he said again, brightly. She paused, now that he was looking at her. 'I can't go back.'

'What do you mean? Where else would you go?'

She had pulled her uniform down around her legs and pressed her knees together, aware of the cold glint of liquid seeping from between her thighs. It was worse than the dentist, the horror of being pitched back in a chair, of having your mouth stretched until it ached and filled with saliva, of not being able to swallow. She looked across at him pleadingly.

'Come on, what is it?'

'What we've just done . . .' She sank back against the seat with the effort of bringing up the words.

'Don't be so serious! There's nothing wrong, is there?'

It was like the clock striking midnight and being returned to pumpkins and mice. She could feel herself flailing, hopelessly trying to reach for a rope, 'But, you can get pregnant, can't you?' The word came out like a word from a dictionary of French or Spanish.

He snorted, reaching for the keys. 'You'll be fine. Trust me.'

'How do you know? It does mean something to you, doesn't it?'

'Of course it does. It was nice. Unexpected.' He turned the key in the ignition with no effect. A second and a third time until the car throbbed into life. He relaxed visibly and felt for the gear stick.

'But what happened?'

He paused and Alison thought for a second there was still a chance to turn everything right, for him to take her and hold her and pop the question and spell out their future.

'Little Miss Muffet!' he said, half affectionately, half in disbelief. He was craning round, reversing down the track.

'You can't joke about it!'

'I'm not joking. Come on, don't be so serious.'

It was a line that cut her dead, the razor edge of a blade. She put her finger to it.

'How can you say that?'

'Say what?'

'Not to be serious.'

'Oh, come on – We both knew what we were doing.'

'But I wouldn't have, unless . . .'

'Unless what?'

'Unless I thought there was something in it.'

He looked at her then for the first time with a trace of worry about his mouth, wrenching the car into first gear. 'What? Money?'

'What do you mean! What on earth do you mean? How dare you!'

'Calm down. Joke.'

'It's not a joke. How dare you say that – I can't believe you'd say that!'

'It was a joke. Sorry. Calm down. Look, I didn't ask for this. Come on. Let's just get home.'

The trees along the side of the road were passing in a blur. Alison bit into her lip until she could taste the metal of her own blood. She was torn between wanting to open the door and throw herself spinning out of the car down into the valley and the persistent speck of a hope that he must somehow come round; that if she kept her head she could still manage to salvage things. 'I only did it because . . . because I thought you might feel something for me.'

'I hardly know you! But,' he added hastily, 'I like you. You're all right. Of course I do.'

'You only go to bed with people you love.'

'We weren't in bed.'

'What we did!'

'It's not Sunday school. This is the modern world. You're a nurse aren't you?'

'You can't be like this,' Alison said, raising her voice again, cutting herself everywhere she turned. It was like trying to hold up the sea wall, keeping herself together, and she was shaking with the effort. 'Eileen . . .'

'Look,' he said all of a sudden, glancing up at his mirror, 'forget it. Don't bring Eileen into it. It's got nothing to do with her. Let's just say it never happened. I was naughty; I read the signs wrong. Let's forget it. You're a nice girl. I like you. But don't get all mad on me. It's between you and me. Put it down to experience. Come on, let's get you back.'

*

Her head is pounding and her throat raw from where she's been breathing through her mouth. After a while, she lifts herself and inspects her son's room: his bed, its duvet flung back, the top drawer of the chest agape, cleared out of socks and pants and vests: after-the-horse-has-bolted. Her nose is tight where the blood has dried, delicately and inconclusively plugged, and she holds her head carefully as she gets up to look on the desk. Immediately she sees the page set there, torn out from a spiral-bound book, held in place with a mug of old tea, and addressed to her:

Mother
Mr H says I can kip over the shop. Better go – let things settle down. Don't fret – Will ring. Rob.

It was out. He had gone. He had gone.

LIZZIE

32

Lizzie slept, or pretended to sleep most of the way back. They'd discussed staying on, but there was no point, she said. Wakefully she raged to herself, eating herself up with it, him taking her away only to rub her nose in it, to make it irretrievably worse.

She must have nodded off because when she tried to open them, her eyes were glued together; she wiped her mouth and pulled herself round in the seat belt, recognising with a shock how close they were to home.

As soon as they drew up, Biddy, with second sight, came running out of the front door. 'Mummy! Have you got us a present?' She was jumping up and down, so pretty with her short fringe and long thick hair, her flesh like sweeties, it almost made Lizzie cry. Then Amelia hearing the commotion came out looking disgruntled, standing four-square against her. Jack as usual was nowhere to be seen. When he appeared, she thought, with a stab of missing him again, it was like a near extinct creature stumbling into the camp, a glimpse was a gift that you'd wait up for all night.

Amelia was twisting the toe of her sandal into the road chippings. 'I thought you were coming back tomorrow?'

In an instant she was inflamed. Any thought she'd harboured of coming home to them and making it better turned sour. It was as if each one of them, by the way they had secretly grown without her, their careless reception, was staving her off. And the unexpected quarter of their rejection only heightened her despair and fuelled her anger, arming herself against them, telling herself that every one of them in their own way had robbed her. She wanted to fold them all back in, to live again, to be loved for herself and not just as the bearer and the slave of these children that were his; she wanted to be looked at with fire, to be set alight; not this slow, inexorable suffocation.

John looked pained and older. There were three new white flecks in his beard.

'Have you had a nice time?' Lizzie asked.

Biddy was still pestering, grabbing at their bags. 'Have you got us a present, Mummy?'

'Did *you* have a nice time?' Amelia asked sarcastically. Lizzie looked at John and he jerked as if a fly had landed on him. 'It was fine, wasn't it?' he said, without elaborating.

It was just a matter of holding out, for a few hours perhaps, of keeping calm, of not rising to things. Ruth, when she appeared, looked bashful, crushed even and Lizzie wondered if she was to blame somehow for the way Ruth had turned out, hunching her shoulders, just like she caught herself doing, apologising.

'Amelia says you've got a boyfriend—'

'She's a liar!'

'Never mind.'

'She's a stupid liar.'

'It's all right, Ruth, she's only teasing.'

'She's a bitch.'

Lizzie was irritable and didn't want distracting from her own grievances. 'Come on, I was only asking.'

'You can't deny it,' Amelia said.

'She's gone bright red,' Biddy pointed out, hugging herself.

RUTH

33

There was part of me that was pathetically grateful for Amelia's reading of the situation, clutching at the straw that because she might believe it to be true, it could be. At the same time, I had to concentrate wholeheartedly on denying it: denying it because I wanted it to be true or because it patently wasn't true.

'I thought you were coming back tomorrow?'

Mummy looked at Daddy, empty-handed. *Why couldn't she just answer a question without having to refer to him?* Eventually she said lamely, 'We missed you. We'd finished; it was raining; there was nothing more to see or do.'

Everything she said had a mechanical ring to it and a reaching out for him to back her up, but he didn't respond. He looked as if he was already sick of being back.

'We had ghosts . . . when you were gone,' Biddy said, her eyes wide.

'Did you? Where?'

'They were downstairs, making noises in the middle of the night.'

'Did you?' Mummy looked at me.

'So she says . . .'

'Well, what was it?'

'Who knows? Ghosts.'

'Were you scared, Biddy?'

'Yes, I *was* scared.'

'No, she wasn't.'

'I was!'

'We're back now, darling, aren't we? There won't be any ghosts tonight.'

'Is it true that the ladies died downstairs?'

'No. No. It isn't. They were taken away. They probably died in hospital. Who's been telling you stories? Anyway, we're back now. What are we having for supper? Ruth? Are you cooking for us? What have you been eating while we were away?'

'Beans,' Biddy sang. 'Beans means Heinz.'

'Let's have pasta, shall we? All right?'

They left us to do the washing-up on our own. When we'd finished, we came upstairs. Mummy was glaring into a book. She wouldn't have the telly on, even to look, and Amelia began to argue with her, 'Why not?'

'Because I say so.'

'But why?'

'If you've got nothing better to do, go to bed.'

Biddy crossed her arms and began kicking Jack from her side of the sofa.

'Leave him alone.'

Amelia piped up, 'If you let us watch telly we won't fight.'

'I'm not discussing it.'

'But otherwise we'll fight, we've nothing else to do.'

'Go to bed then. Read a book; don't be so bloody gormless.'

'Mrs Saunders says that grown-ups shouldn't swear at children . . .'

'Don't speak to me like that. I say what I like. Go to bed.'

Suddenly, Daddy rose up out of his chair, dislodging the catalogue that was perched on its arm. He made a noise like a shell coming over, whistling before it lands, 'For Christ's sake, is there no peace?' and he marched out leaving us suspended in his wake. All except Mummy, who, a few minutes later, stirred herself, pulling on her sandals and growling at us, as if it was all our fault, 'Stay here.'

LIZZIE

34

The early evening, as it so often did, gave itself up to golden sunshine, but Lizzie wasn't interested. All along the road she was rehearsing what she was going to say, her hand by her side beating her words like eggs. She knew where he was headed and she knew he'd already given himself up, he would be talking, negotiating, reassuring the face on the other end of the line in that coaxing voice she'd long ago forgotten the sound of.

Whatever she was going to say, she knew she had lost. All she could see was the red of the phone box, as if the tears in her eyes were blood red, and the whole world tinted with the smear of them. When she got there, the paint was so thick and shiny it looked wet, as if it would come off in her hands and fingers if she touched it. He turned his blank face over his shoulder and seemed to look straight through her. She slapped the box with the flat of her hand. 'Let me in! Open the door! Let me in!' She wanted to damage him, to pull his hair, to batter him. 'Get out! Get out here!'

John stuck to the receiver until the last minute, talking, talking before he had to give it up, letting it drop in his agitation, bending, listening again and hanging it back in its cradle reluctantly. As he put his shoulder to the door, his arms were poised to lift about his head. When he looked at her, it was from a bridge, as though he knew the last line had been cut, that he could watch her cry and swear and threaten, and she no longer had the power to take him with her; he only had to stand his ground for her to be rushed along by a current that was all the time careering her further away. Lizzie swore to kill him and herself, again and again and again, unless he came with her, but her voice was becoming fainter and fainter: it had no sting, no power over him at all, the chatter of a bird. If he kept his nerve, eventually she'd drop altogether from view and become part of the general racket from which he had found an extraordinary and bewildering reprieve.

RUTH

35

We were bundled into the window in the little room at the side of the cottage, trying to get headroom. If you'd seen us from the road, we'd have looked flat, like a kite trapped in the branches of the house, fixed by a single string to Mummy who was stamping off to find someone to get us down.

When Daddy finally came out, his arms were raised around his head to block his ears. Although she was shouting at him, they seemed to be gradually working their way towards us, her skittering backwards and forwards and him inching along, head down. We got ourselves back into the living room, with books opened, Jack's upside down, Biddy disentangling wool, when we heard Mummy at the front door.

'Where's Daddy?' Biddy asked her as she stepped into the room.

'I've no idea.' Her voice sounded dull and dead.

'When's he coming back?' Amelia said.

'Get out, all of you. Go to bed.'

'But it's not time.'

'Do what I say.'

We looked at each other and none of us moved.

'Do it!' She scrawled the words, loading them with spit, 'Do it, now!' as if she would scratch our faces off, as if the four of us were just the bits and pieces of him she wanted to kill.

This time we didn't move because we heard the judder and thud of the front door: Daddy striding in and downstairs to the kitchen. Mummy was crouched motionless on the carpet, very slightly mouthing a conversation to herself, but her eyes swivelled instantly to the floor, as if she was alive to his every move. She picked herself up and went dumbly, blindly after him. We heard her missing a step near the bottom, stumbling like a dropped stitch.

'Is it because of Batman?' Jack hissed at me, folding into himself. 'Did you tell?'

'What?' Amelia leapt on him. 'What about Batman?'

'Shut up, I want to hear.'

'Who's Batman?'

'It doesn't matter. Shut up!'

'Batman's dead,' Jack said slowly, as if he'd only just admitted it.

Amelia opened her eyes so wide, they filled her glasses. 'Who's Batman? Who does he mean?'

'Be quiet!'

'Does he mean the brother?'

'No. It's a calf.'

'A calf called Batman?'

'Amelia, shut up!'

'What happened to it?'

'Drowned.'

'God! How?'

'Jack.'

'I didn't! It wasn't my fault. I didn't do it!'

'How did he do it?'

'It got in the pond.'

'Did they know it was Jack?'

'It wasn't me! I didn't do it!'

'Is that what they're rowing about?'

'No.'

'What then?'

The voices were a mumble, painstakingly quiet. My ears hurt with the strain of trying to make out words.

We could hear Daddy, in a slightly raised, spelling-it-out voice. 'She's ill. There's nothing I can do. I have to go.'

And Mummy, outraged, 'I'm ill. Anyone can be ill.'

'She's in hospital.'

'With what?'

'It doesn't matter. The fact is I have to go.'

'I don't believe she's really ill. What proof have you got?'

'I don't need proof.'

'If you go now – I mean it, it's the end.'

The silence that followed was like a vacuum as if nothing could possibly survive down there. Suddenly without warning the downstairs door heaved open and Biddy blundered in, singing to herself. She went straight into the kitchen and was swallowed up in the hush. Then we heard her voice, reproachful, belligerent. And Mummy's rang out loud and accusing, 'Why don't you tell her the truth? You bloody tell her!'

'Oh God,' Amelia said under her breath.

By now we were squeezed together in the doorway, hanging out over the landing. I had hold of Amelia's wrist.

We heard the scrape of a kitchen chair and Daddy clearing his throat. When he spoke, it was in a kneeling-down voice. I thought I knew what he was going to say before he even began, like anticipating the potholes in the road biking up to the post box. We would believe him when he said he wasn't going anywhere, that everything would be fine, that Mummy was mad and everything would calm down and not to worry. And the tone of his voice wrong-footed us for a moment. 'Listen,' he said, 'I won't go far. Don't worry. I love you, just the same . . .'

'But where are you going?'

'Not far, I promise . . . Come on, don't cry. Come here, sweetie.'

'But why are you going away?'

'It's just for a bit, just so we can sort things out . . .'

'Tell her the truth!'

'Look, sweetie, don't worry, I'll still be able to see you . . .'

'Stop lying to her.'

'I'm not lying.'

'Biddy, he's leaving, he's leaving all of us and he isn't coming back.'

'For Christ's sake, Lizzie, it doesn't have to be like this.'

'Yes, it does. You're going, aren't you? You're going off to live with her. You're leaving us for her. You can't dress it up any other way. Just tell them the truth.'

He didn't say any more and his silence flashed over us like white light.

I never willingly looked at Amelia, unless it was to count how many spots she had relative to mine or how greasy her hair was. But when I looked at her now I was shocked to find how closely her expression mirrored mine, it was as if we'd blossomed and died at the same time. We knew we were supposed to cry, but we couldn't. Biddy was whimpering, but still we couldn't. We were embarrassed by the moment, one of those moments when something happens and you don't know what to do. We looked at each other and I was filled with an overwhelming sense of contrition for all the terrible things I'd said and thought, seeing her face which was usually so adamant, now uncertain, unsure of which way to go. We held on by the wrists looking so hard that in the end our mouths began to curl. All we could think of was the impossibility of trying not to laugh. It was too late: our shoulders began to shake and we creased up, hysterically clutching on to each other like two drunken sailors caught in the act.

36

I try to remember his exact words when he said goodbye to us. Although it was as if he would come back, this time I couldn't picture him actually saying so. He didn't take the car, either. He had a bag and he was walking to Ellersdale to get the bus, to get to Hexham, to get the train. It felt like a dream. Like being a different person in a dream.

I went to Mummy when he'd gone. I told her about the calf. I told her I thought she needed to go down to see the Burdens, to say sorry; that Jack didn't know how. She was looking firmly at the floor. Then she said, lifting her head with a flounce, 'Don't criticise.'

'I'm not, I'm just saying.'

She smiled a cold pat smile. 'Don't try and tell me how to be a mother.'

'I'm not.'

'I'm perfectly capable of taking him down there without you telling me, thank you.'

I watched her through the window going out to speak to Jack on the swing, joggling the arm of it, persuading him to come with her, holding out her hand.

LIZZIE

37

Alison is there in the reluctant opening of the door. They must be a similar age, Lizzie thinks, but in her manner Alison seems at least a generation older. She has the shape of one of those crochet dolls: no distinguishable difference between her bust and her hips. Her hair is scraped up out of the way. For the first time Lizzie notices an intricate network of veins around the tops of her cheeks and her nose like lights from a city a hundred miles away. She looks washed out, bothered.

'Alison,' Lizzie is holding Jack's hand tightly; it is like a flipper, unbending in her grasp. 'We've come to say sorry.'

Alison looks as if she doesn't understand. 'There's no need—'

'Please, Jack wants to.' Lizzie nudges him forward. 'Don't you?'

Alison shakes her head and says, 'There's no need, really.' Then reluctantly, because Lizzie is standing her ground, 'Would you like to come in?'

Lizzie locks her with an anxious smile. 'That would be nice, thank you. He thinks you won't want him to help here any more,' she says, following Alison inside.

'Oh no. Not at all. It's all right. Don't let him fret about it.'

'If we can do anything. I know it must have been worth something to you, a calf I mean, in money terms . . .'

'No, no, he wouldn't hear of it. Please don't mention it. It's over with.'

'Are you sure? Really? Jack is so, so sorry, aren't you, Jack? I know he's been terribly worried about it.'

He wriggles out of her grasp. 'Can I go now?'

'Oh, Jack! Go on then!'

He is gone like a fish released.

Alison stands against the stove and taps a cigarette packet nervously on the enamel, staving off the moment to get one out.

'Would you mind if I had one?' Lizzie asks.

'Oh – of course. I'm sorry, yes, of course.'

Alison tweaks one out for herself too and strikes a match, holding it in front of Lizzie's eyes. Lizzie puts the end of the cigarette in her mouth and draws her lips unnaturally small around it. Alison makes a popping sound lighting her own, takes a long drag.

Even though Lizzie has sat down, the cigarette goes straight to her head and she feels as if she is falling backwards, her hands unaccountably shaky. There's a small photograph on the dresser at eye level and she latches onto it. It's a picture of two boys in shorts, one of them on a tricycle, the other, the bigger one, standing; both of them looking at the camera, the standing one, wrinkling his face up, the one on the bike grinning out. She thinks how alike little boys can be, their knees, the length of their shins, the place where the legs of their shorts meet their thighs, their bony shoulders. Just like Jack, either one of them.

'I meant to say before, when I heard about your son. I meant to come and say how desperately sorry I was – we were – but we didn't realise until a while after it happened and then it seemed too late to say anything. I really am so sorry about it.'

Alison took a long drag and wobbled visibly, her two eyes on jets of air. 'Thank you.'

Lizzie puffed out a clap of smoke. They both sat staring ahead.

'It must be the most terrible thing, to lose a child – to lose anyone,' Lizzie proffered after a while. 'It hasn't happened to me, not yet; I suppose I've been lucky.' Alison was fiddling with the table top scratching at a dried splash of food with her nail. 'It happens to all of us at one time or another, parents and whatnot, we just have to get used to it, I suppose.'

'I wonder if you ever do?'

They drew on their cigarettes again and Lizzie gazed into the vat of smoke they were brewing between them, Alison's refined by her lungs into a continuous stream, hers inept as wool along wire. There was a strange familiarity between the two of them – Alison felt it – part of her wishing Lizzie away, the other part curiously grateful for that fact that she was sitting there, as if she had indeed known her for years, as if she had come to make amends.

'I don't know if Jack ever says anything to you, or Ruth? It's not been a terribly good summer for us – you might have gathered?'

Alison shook her head. 'I'm sorry . . .'

'Don't be. It's nothing to what you must have been through, but sometimes, you know, I've thought – and maybe this sounds terrible – but that it might be better to have someone die, rather than them just go. It might be a better way: then you can grieve and you know what you're grieving for.'

Alison hardly moved except to tap the ash. She could exist on so little air. When she did speak it came out harder than she meant it. 'It must depend on who's dying and who's going – and how.'

'Yes. Oh God, I'm so sorry. I'm being ridiculous. It's just . . .' and Lizzie gulped hard. 'I didn't mean it like that. It's so – so difficult at the moment, you know, it would be easier to accept . . .'

There was a single tear like a curtain pull down one cheek, and then the other. For one strange moment, Alison felt light-headed, as if she were floating, as if she could look down and see the upturn of Lizzie's pale tear-stained face. *What a naughty boy was that to try to drown poor pussy cat?*

'If I think about it,' Lizzie sniffed, 'I can't be sure we'll ever come back here, not after this – if it turns out that he's done what he's said he's going to do . . . But I did want to come in any case and say thank you, thank you for looking after the children. With all you've had on your plate. And how really, really sorry I am. I know I shouldn't have asked you . . .'

It was hardly perceptible, but it might have looked to Lizzie then as if Alison made a very tentative move of her fingers across the table towards her.

'You've been so kind,' Lizzie said, wiping her cheeks with the edge of her sleeve and easing back her chair. 'It would be nice to stay in touch. I hope – I do hope we stay in touch.'

Alison wasn't listening any longer. To her amazement Lizzie had turned into a stranger, a complete stranger, talking in her faltering, apologetic voice. She couldn't believe her eyes.

'Thank you again,' Lizzie gulped, twisting up at the edges, stubbing out the last half of her cigarette violently into the saucer, thinking, *Don't be nice to me, don't feel sorry for me, you'll make me cry.* 'I can't say how sorry I am about everything.'

RUTH

38

'What did she say?' I ask too eagerly when Mummy gets back.

She looks at me for a minute with her chin out and then says, 'Fine. It's fine with Jack. Leave him alone. It's absolutely fine.'

'But it was right, wasn't it, to go down there, to say sorry?'

'Ruth, will you please stop bossing everyone around. You're not so perfect yourself, you know. Just stop doing it. You're like your father. You're not their bloody mother whatever you think. Just stop getting at me all the time.'

Mummy doesn't stop crying. It isn't sobbing, always, but there's a constant wetness to her face like a glaze. She speaks only to herself, under her breath, as if she's lost something but can't remember what it is or where she's put it. Then she starts on the cleaning. She begins heaving the rag rugs about, collecting them in a heap at the top of the stairs.

Beating the rugs is usually the last job of the summer and the worst, and it's always Daddy – even though he doesn't have anything to do with the cleaning – who makes us do it.

We don't argue with her. Amelia shoves Biddy off the swing, unhooking its rigid seat from the frame and laying it on the grass. She climbs onto the wall and then pulls herself up onto the crossbar of the frame ready to start hauling the rugs over the top, me and Mummy handing one up to her and then dragging it down from the other side.

We stand with a rug hanging between us and, although I am not speaking to her, begin to take alternate shots, backwards and forwards – her with the broom, me with the little brush – each thud loosening a cloud of grit and dust that gets into our eyes and our mouths.

Biddy and Jack hold off, obedient in the face of Mummy's determination, but suddenly Biddy can't contain herself any longer. 'Can I do it? I want to do it.'

'Not now, Biddy, just let us get on with it.'

'But I want to do it.'

'I said, *no*.'

'When's Daddy coming back?'

The rug flumps to a standstill between us.

'Get inside,' Mummy's voice cracks. 'Do what I say.'

Biddy's jaw trembles as she turns to run in. 'You never ask me. You never let me have a go. You never think of me.'

The last rug is the one from in front of the fire. Where the others are made from the greys, browns and blues of everyday jackets and coats jumbled together, this one is carefully plotted. At its centre there's a flaming pattern of scarlet flowers – the tiny flags of red flannel petticoats – chasing each other round. It's so heavy to lift that I have to climb up onto the other side of the frame to help Amelia feed it over; heavy as a body. Before we've even begun, objects loosen from its folds: a button, a paperclip, two elastic bands.

I take the first hit with the back of the brush, shutting my eyes. Then Mummy, launching at it so there's a dull thwack as the head of her broom hits it in the stomach. We go at it alternately like two boxers, Amelia egging us on, with a common enemy between us that we can hit instead of each other. There is no sign that Mummy will let up, huffing the air with each of her blows, sometimes a word buried in it. Her eyes are fixed and blazing so that even though my arms are aching I don't want to be the one to call her off.

We go on as if there will be no end to it, bashing the soft scales of the rug back to the tuftiness and colour of when we first arrived, as if it is a way of turning back the clock; as if time is just dirt; history, dirt. You can see the flowers getting redder and redder and brighter and brighter the more we beat. I can't help it reminding me of Bobbie in *The Railway Children*, refusing to move off the track, waving her flags at the train and, as soot and smoke dissolve in the air, shouting like a knife that rips through every last page of the book, '*Daddy! My Daddy!*'

39

Mummy is on a roll. At teatime we have a Penguin each, but we don't stop. She announces as a challenge that we're leaving: that we must grab our things, our clothes, our toothbrushes, because we're going home.

'Can't we go tomorrow, Mummy? Can't we stay a bit?' Biddy is joggling Arabella on her hip as if the whole of life involves looking after her baby.

'No, we can't. We've no bread, no food, and we need to get back. We're going home. It's decided and there's an end to it. We'll be there when you wake up.'

Later, she is kneeling on the floor over her handbag, which is overflowing with pieces of paper, broken biscuits, biros, old pennies, Tampax, books, jiggling it, stuffing it all in. 'Help me!' Randomly she begins to pick pieces of clothing off the floor. 'Get me another bag, go on, hurry up.' Amelia has stomped into the bedroom and takes the meticulously stacked pile of her clothes and plonks it in the big pink suitcase Mummy and Daddy had when they were married. Mummy is standing over the open boot of the car, exasperated because Biddy is running backwards and forwards handing her bits of china one at a time, half-knitted hats and scarves for her doll, and Jack is asking to bring the field mouse he'd found dried up under the sofa, and a matchbox of woodlice.

'I want clothes. Get your clothes together, and your things, not this stuff – do what I say, please, for once.'

'But what if Daddy comes back and we're not here?' Biddy says.

'He's not coming back. For the last time he is not coming back.'

Usually there are two or three days to get used to the idea of going home. Biddy and Jack don't let up whingeing, but I have no armour to cross her again and bring my own bag out dutifully. Then I am brought up short.

'What have you got there?' I hear her asking Biddy, with sudden interest.

It is too late to intervene and I can only watch in horror as Biddy waves the clasped hands she has pulled from under my bed like a wand.

'Where did you get these?' Mummy snatches at them. 'Where are they from?'

I can see Biddy is a little taken aback and beginning to falter in her story. 'From the garden.'

'Don't lie, Biddy. Come on, tell me where you got them?'

'I did,' and then she adds pointedly, 'from Ruth.'

Mummy swings round, her face aghast. I am caught on the hop, glaring at Biddy, who is petulant. 'It was you.'

'Big mouth!' I hiss uselessly at her.

'Don't speak to her like that! I'm waiting . . .'

I know then that I am lost. 'It was Amelia's fault.'

Amelia appears from behind me like the wicked witch of the west, exultant in her outrage. 'No it wasn't. You liar! You told me—'

'You would've taken them if I hadn't—'

'No, I wouldn't. I never would've. They're from a *grave* – anyone can see that.'

'Is that true? You took them from the graveyard? Ruth! I don't believe you! How could you steal? You're fifteen years old. I shouldn't have to tell you. For God's sake, what on earth did you think you were doing? Why?'

Her voice has turned into a howl and there's nothing I can do or say but let it fall on me, crushing in its accusation.

'You'll have to take them back. Quickly! Now! You'll have to run and put them back where you found them. This minute!'

'But there isn't time.'

'Yes, there is. Go on, do it now.'

'Someone might see.'

'Do it! I don't care. I want them put back. How could you even think of stealing from a graveyard? Hasn't enough happened? Aren't things bad enough for you?'

I was exposed, finally, overturned like a woodlouse obscenely waving its legs in the air, its ugly underbelly for all to see. Always before I had felt there was someone on my side: an Old Gentleman, God, a Grandfather looking down from heaven: someone watching how well I could negotiate a field, how patiently I tolerated everyone. But all I can feel now is the cold and furious gaze of someone washing their hands of me, running me to ground.

In the lane there is the first mizzle of rain. When I get to the bottom of the hill it starts properly. The graveyard looks forbidding on the other side of the bridge, hunched and dour. It seems futile even to attempt to put the hands back, like returning a long-cold egg to its nest. I stand, leaning over the coarse stone of the bridge, looking out along the length of the river pitted with rain, circles within circles, hurrying endlessly on and over, its quirks and its jumps, eating into the bank for something to do, oblivious of time or season or history or who loves whom.

Hardly turning I glance furtively towards the farmyard. There's no truck, no sign of life at all, the windows like a strip of negatives. I open my fingers and let the hands drop unpremeditated from my grasp; a splash as they hit the brown enveloping water. Perhaps they bob up further on, a bubble of air carrying them towards Ellershead, waving as they pass, like the queen, or clapping at themselves for having finally got away. Because I know it would make no possible difference putting them back now, that I'm not being watched any longer, only being left, part of the dirt, the mess.

My plimsolls weld themselves to the ground; I stick and unstick myself all the way back up the hill, the rain plastering my jeans to my legs, releasing from each drop the *I told you so* of its lesson: that the person you really are is the person you are left with when you're not wanted, not by anyone: by Amelia, Biddy, Jack, by Mummy, by Daddy, by Robert, by anyone; ever. That is the core of you: the unwanted person.

It is only when I get as far as the steps up to the cottage that I hear, like a cow, or a foghorn, 'Roo! Roo!' The noise unravels itself gradually into a human sound, a word being wrung out, 'Ruth! Ruth!' Like waving a lost glove or an odd sock. '*Ruth*! Where are you? Ruth! We're going! *Ruth!*' This time it is thrown so hard and furiously that when it reaches me it's like a blow and the words in my throat fly out before I have a chance to think: 'I'm here!'

GRAHAM

40

Before he reached home Graham drew in to where the phone box was and stared out blankly over the steering wheel into the drizzle. Then he turned off the engine and jumped out, slamming the door of the truck, heading off on foot up to the tops. The wind was in his face as he climbed, recriminatory one minute, mournful the next, like a finger sounding around the rim of the valley. It took him fifteen steady minutes to get as far as the old shooting hut, where he and his brother Ed used to beat for Lord Ellersdale and he stood steadying himself against it, looking out across the valley, picking out the boundaries of the farm, thinking how everything was always a fight, the ground re-arming itself every year with its bogs, its craggy places, its thick, unyielding ground.

The day he'd discovered Eddie, he'd been sent out miserable and cold, checking on sheep in the lower field, looking in at the barn because there were half a dozen missing . . .

At the entrance, Eddie's jacket folded carefully on the floor, its zip like a slow worm. Gloomy out of the daylight, but movement at the other end. Not surprised to see the glow of fleece from sheep who'd barged in to escape the rain. But something else too. Where the joists in the ceiling are bare, a large sack suspended, hanging; closer — tutting at the animals — what he's seeing is not a sack but a body, a head thrown back, eyes rolled, the pattern a rope cuts, hair, the soft, blond girl's hair of him,

drooping forward like a wig, stomach pulled up, out of the rim of a belt
– father's belt – a reek of fundament, a terrible reek, and heavy boots
nudged like a mobile by guilty-looking sheep.

It had not been a reason to stop. Five generations pouring themselves into those acres which threw up their thistles – the same thistles – year upon year. The quirks of the lie of a field, the dropped hinge of a gate, these things were ingrained and familiar to him as the set of a nose or a chin in a family album. Looking out now to the implacable surface of the hundreds of versions of green and ochre that shifted and danced in front of his eyes, he had the impression of quicksand, gobbling over the bodies and the bones, the toil and the sweat. Standing there, it was as if he was nothing but a tear in the fabric of the landscape through which all the stuffing of anyone around him had been pulled.

Until it came to her – the pull at his loins every time the bull was set among the cows – and realising that what he had craved was not her prettiness (which had seemed unreachable) or her lightness (though that had been a part of it), but more than that: her sinfulness, which meant that she was grateful to be taken in; which made her damaged in a way that matched his own sense of damage; which would keep her there, because she was not worth taking from him.

He dropped to his knees as if his legs had been blasted from under him, the dampness seeping through like patches, shuffling forward on his stumps, wanting to take the earth and cram his mouth with it, or to shout with the filth that was already in there, but with no idea how to form the words, or to whom.

That calf, its slick black hide. It was not only Daniel. Something of it had reminded him of Eddie and then of Robert (the way he wore that jacket as a badge of his difference, day in, day out). It was like a cloud passing overhead: the chill of comprehending for that brief moment the irresistible urge to quit.

ALISON

41

The hail is like bullets. Alison is looking outside to see what on earth has brought it on. She sees Ruth on the bridge, watches her hesitate for a while before turning away up the road, toiling up the hill out of sight. The curtain, which is still drawn, drops back and the kitchen is dusk again. Alison feels her way to the table and sits down. The sight of the girl bending under the rain has made her want to cry. She reaches out for the packet of cigarettes. *Don't get rushed into anything*, she thinks. *You've your whole life ahead of you.* The girl was pretty and you could see she didn't know it. That got you into trouble. It made you grateful for what you could get. It made you accept things when maybe you should have questioned them. Ruth: she suited her name. And with a pang, as Alison drew on the cigarette, she thought, *it might as well have been my name, that: Ruth.* And if she could, she felt she would have swapped with her then and there. All the regret, all the ruefulness – she'd had enough for two lifetimes. What a name to live with, she thought. What a name to give a child.

She is taken unawares by the stillness inside the house and the emptiness. As if whatever drove it has been thrown off its axis, the mill wheel wrenched from the river. It is a strangely familiar feeling come to roost.

Watching him grow – his questioning face that thought it had the measure of her. He had a way about him that wouldn't let her off the hook, that kept her always on her mettle. '*Mother!*' he would say in mock horror, if she argued with him, even if she told him to move his stuff off the kitchen table or to stop pinching her cigarettes. Daniel had been the real baby; in her dreams Robert had been born already speaking to her.

She drew the curtains in the front room and began to lay a fire, moved the big armchair towards the hearth. When she heard the front door, she had already been waiting half an hour longer than she'd expected and she called anxiously to the kitchen where she could hear Graham shaking off his jacket, putting things away in cupboards. He came through with the paper and she watched him as he sat uncomfortably and loosened the laces on his boots.

The only nice thing her mother had ever said about him when she showed her the small grey photograph of their wedding, was how skinny he was and how he looked a little like Fred Astaire, wiry, and Alison had stopped herself saying out loud, not meanly, but because she knew him better, *Pity he couldn't dance*! His face was held together by lines now, weatherbeaten, hung in a way that leaked disappointment.

She couldn't bear to hurt him again, she caught herself thinking, looking at him, bent over in the chair. The thought surprised her, like a drop of rain, cold and mobile, finding its way under a hat through to her scalp. She went over to him and stood just by the arm. His hair was grizzled and damp where it was thinning on the high peak of his head, burnt to a bruise by the sun. He seemed to be reading. She waited.

Then she held on to the arm of the chair and knelt down awkwardly beside him. He didn't register her at first, but looked away, down at the fire, a film of water on his eyes reflecting the flames. Her hand was moving all the time, reaching out towards his. He lifted the paper from his lap and let it fall to the ground. He had let her touch him like a pet. Her fingers moved around his. She couldn't remember having held his hand ever. The skin was rough around his knuckles, like the skin of turnips, and splintering round his nails. Turning his head a fraction, his eyes furiously burning from the fire and seeming to water with the heat, he returned her hold suddenly and tightly.

She had her thumb pressed to his wrist, feeling the blood hopping in its veins, keeping a hold to stop herself from fainting. There had been nothing worse than keeping the knowing and the not knowing apart and it was clear to her that the splinter that had been so deeply buried right from the beginning had finally worked its way to the surface. It didn't matter any longer.

Very slowly, she let her head sink towards his knee and lay waiting – it seemed for ever – to see what he would do. When his hand came hovering above her it was like electricity; she stayed quite still – swallowing once, twice – until he let it go, cupping her ear like a giant shell with the boom boom boom of the sea.

RUTH: Postscript

42

Only Amelia ever went back. She got annoyed when I asked her too specifically how or if things had changed. As far as she could tell, she said, the Burdens were still there, though she didn't see them. And in the graveyard, which was trim and neat, there were new names: Frank Spark, who we'd known, cut into the stone below his wife Elsie, and then, set flat on a marble plaque in the ground, Daniel Burden, with his dates and *In Loving Memory*.

Amelia was cross because she thought I wouldn't let it go and she wondered, since I was so keen to find out, why I didn't just go back there myself. I told her, *when a family ends there is nowhere to go back to. All that is left is the archaeology of it, picking over the disappointing traces of a villa or a Roman fort. It shouldn't be like a death, but somehow it is. Not an individual death, but the death of a way of life and of being and of continuing to be . . .*

It is the hardest thing I've had to learn, losing things; so hard to stop the business of looking, of acquiring at all costs, to make good the loss. The others have all got families of their own. My father had more children; Mummy eventually found someone else. I don't know quite what happened to me: nothing ever seemed to work out. I've moved about a bit in jobs – Birmingham, Bradford, West Norwood, Forest Hill – I suppose I find it hard to settle, to feel that anywhere is home. It takes four car loads of boxes, suitcases and bin liners to move because I'm still so bad at throwing stuff out.

It was me that ended up with that black dress of Mrs Brown's, hanging in one wardrobe or another, still there now under a coat. I've tried it on in the past: the waist is too high, the hemline wavy. But I caught myself thinking, *If I hold onto it for when I'm old, when I've shrunk a bit, it might just fit.* Perhaps it was then that the penny began to drop, that I began to question whether I should be making more of an effort to sort things out.

Then I saw an article in a colour magazine about artists who wrap up tracts of landscape, bridges, stretches of coast, trees even. They have produced written instructions that can be followed, detailing fabric for the purpose, special guns to fire fasteners and studs, clips to secure rope to rock. It seemed such a perfect idea, to make a present and a memorial at the same time.

I drew up my own specifications, more in keeping with the place, aiming to create a dome, a huge glass dome that would sit tight over the moor, and through which the distant faces of our family would shine like porcelain dolls. The truth is I was trained so well to ransack that I never lost the habit, scavenging the dump for bits and pieces from this time and that, from one person or another, to fill in the gaps. So much material, it began to take on a life: Graham, Alison, Lizzie, I hope they will forgive me for the words I've put into their mouths, sitting here with my old records turning, willing for it all to happen in a certain way (the smoke to clear from the platform, the shout to erupt that will make it all right).

I hope I've got beyond that. In the end all that is important to me is to say that it happened, not necessarily in that order, not necessarily like that. It reminds me of learning the Lord's Prayer. I was so proud to have it by heart, *Our Father* . . . At one time I thought it was what made the world go round, and I still hear myself repeat it when called upon *for ever and ever* just as I did when I was a child. The comfort lies in the fact that it is still there, intact, even though I don't believe a word of it, not any more, not for a minute.

Acknowledgements

A huge thank you to Jessica Feaver and Carol Hughes for patient readings from the start, to Peter Straus and Rowan Routh for perseverance and encouragement, to James Gurbutt for his astute editorial guidance, to Vicki Feaver for her example and to Clare and Michael Morpurgo, for their forbearance and friendship.

An early extract from the novel appeared under the title, 'The Art of Losing' in *NW14*, edited by Lavinia Greenlaw and Helon Habila (Granta, 2006).